SUMMER SMART

Grade

3 • 4

Special thanks are given to
Vikalp Jain, Dev Patel, Tiffany Feler, Erica Ho,** and **Marco Chang
for their involvement in the Arts & Crafts Section.

Printed in Canada

Contents

Grade 3–4

Mathematics

Social Studies

Arts & Crafts

A. **The children collect cans for their community. Read what they say and help them find out how many cans they will collect after 6 days. Then fill in the blank.**

1. 

I have collected 79 cans already. I think I will collect 1 can each day from now on.

Day	1	2	3	4	5	6
No. of Cans in All	80					

2. 

I have collected 90 cans already. I think I will collect 2 cans each day from now on.

Day	1	2	3	4	5	6
No. of Cans in All	92					

3. 

I have collected 80 cans already. I think I will collect 5 cans each day from now on.

Day	1	2	3	4	5	6
No. of Cans in All	85					

4. 

I have collected 25 cans already. I think I will collect 25 cans each day from now on.

Day	1	2	3	4	5	6
No. of Cans in All	50					

5. ________________ will collect the most cans after 6 days.

B. Read what the children say. Help them solve the problems.

1.

My goal is to collect 500 cans. I've collected 427 cans. How many more cans do I need to meet my goal?

________________ = ________ ________ more

2.

I've collected 273 pop cans and 185 beer cans. How many cans have I collected in all?

________________ = ________ ________ cans

3.

If I collect 25 more cans, I will have 400 cans in all. How many cans have I collected?

________________ = ________ ________ cans

4.

I've collected 577 cans. 129 of them were picked in the park. How many cans were not picked in the park?

________________ = ________ ________ cans

5.

Last year I collected 415 cans. This year I collected 98 more than last year. How many cans did I collect this year?

________________ = ________ ________ cans

C. **Mrs. Philips uses a circle graph to show how many cans each group of children collected. Look at the circle graph. Answer the questions.**

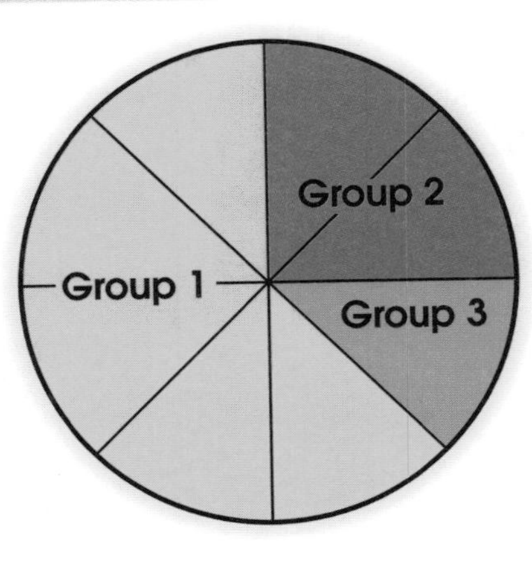

1. Which group collected the most cans? ____________
2. Which group collected the fewest cans? ____________
3. If Group 3 collected 100 cans, how many cans did
   a. Group 2 collect? ____________
   b. Group 1 collect? ____________
4. Check ✔ the bar graph that best shows the information on the circle graph above.

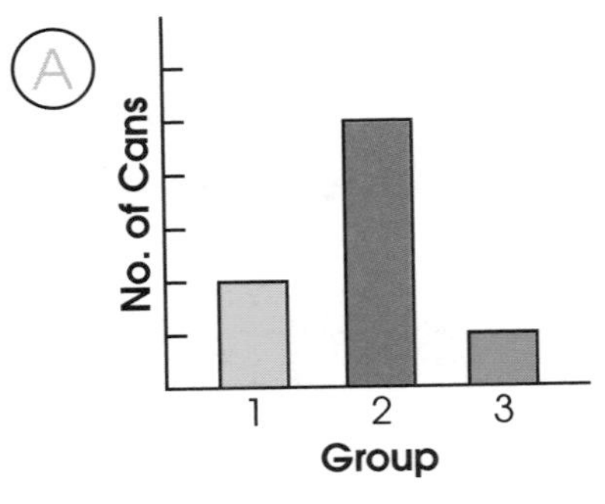

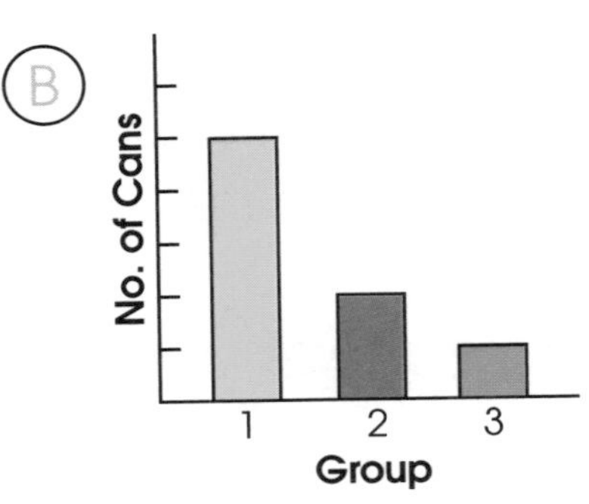

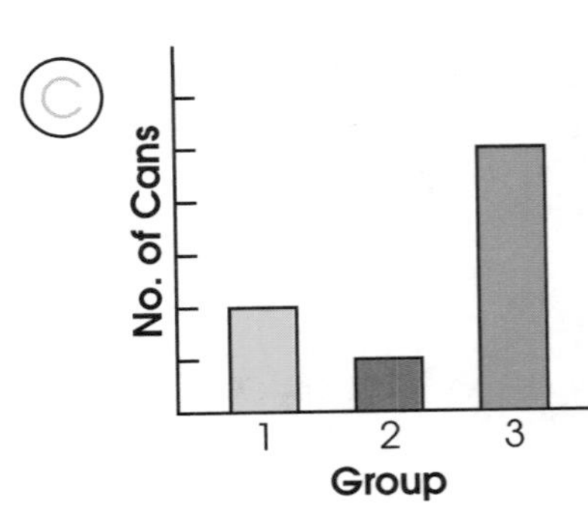

Week 1

MATHEMATICS

D. The children help Mrs. Philips put the cans into boxes. See how they put the cans. Draw the cans and find the numbers.

1. $\frac{1}{3}$ of a box of cans have 5 cans. How many cans are there in a box?

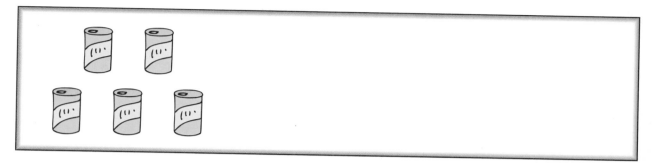

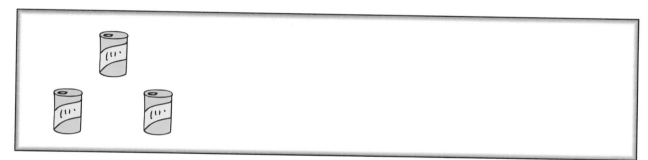

There are ________ cans in a box.

2. $\frac{1}{4}$ of a box of cans have 3 cans. How many cans are there in a box?

There are ________ cans in a box.

Solve the problem.

A fish tank is half-filled with water. After taking out 2 L of water, Jane needs to pour in 6 L of water to fill up the tank. What is the capacity of the tank?

The capacity of the tank is ________ L.

Week 1

ENGLISH

Marco loved magic. He used all sorts of books and props to learn how to perform magic tricks. His family suggested that he put on a show for his friends and neighbours. Marco thought it was a great idea.

Marco's sister, Rosa, made beautiful, bright signs that she posted around the neighbourhood. Marco's dad helped him get the backyard ready. Together, they built a small stage and used old sheets for curtains. Marco's mom decided to make chocolate chip cookies and pink lemonade to serve to the audience.

The backyard was packed on the day of the show. Rosa acted as Marco's assistant. She welcomed the guests and announced, "Ladies and gentlemen, boys and girls, I now present to you Marco the Magician!" The crowd applauded loudly as Marco burst through the curtains onto the stage. He entertained the audience with card tricks and some of his jokes. He waved his magic wand and "PRESTO" – a white rabbit was pulled from his hat. Marco even made Rosa disappear and then with one simple "ABRACADABRA", she was back!

After the show, the audience enjoyed the delicious refreshments prepared by Marco's mom. As they left, they congratulated Marco and told him they would be back for his next show.

A. Put the events in order. Write 1 to 8.

_____ Marco made his sister disappear.

_____ Marco's mother baked cookies and made lemonade.

_____ Rosa made signs for the show.

_____ Marco and his father built a stage in the backyard.

_____ The neighbours congratulated Marco after the show.

_____ Marco pulled a rabbit from his hat.

_____ Rosa welcomed the guests.

_____ Rosa reappeared.

B. Read each paragraph. Put a line through the sentence that does not belong.

1. Marco loves magic. He learned magic tricks by reading books and practising. A magician usually wears a top hat. In last year's Christmas show, Marco put on a spectacular performance and everyone loved his show, especially the one with a puppy coming out from an empty backpack.

2. Marco's sister, Rosa, is a great helper to Marco. Although she does not know how to perform magic tricks, she helps her brother with decorating the stage, preparing the props, and assisting him in the show. Rosa has made a huge poster for the upcoming magic show for their neighbours. The show will be held in their backyard. Their parents will help out too. Rosa's puppy doesn't like cookies.

C. Write complete sentences using the following words.

1. invisible

____

2. surprised

____

3. impossible

____

4. suddenly

____

5. magician

____

D. Match the words from the hat on the left with those words in the hat on the right to make compound words. Write the new words on the lines.

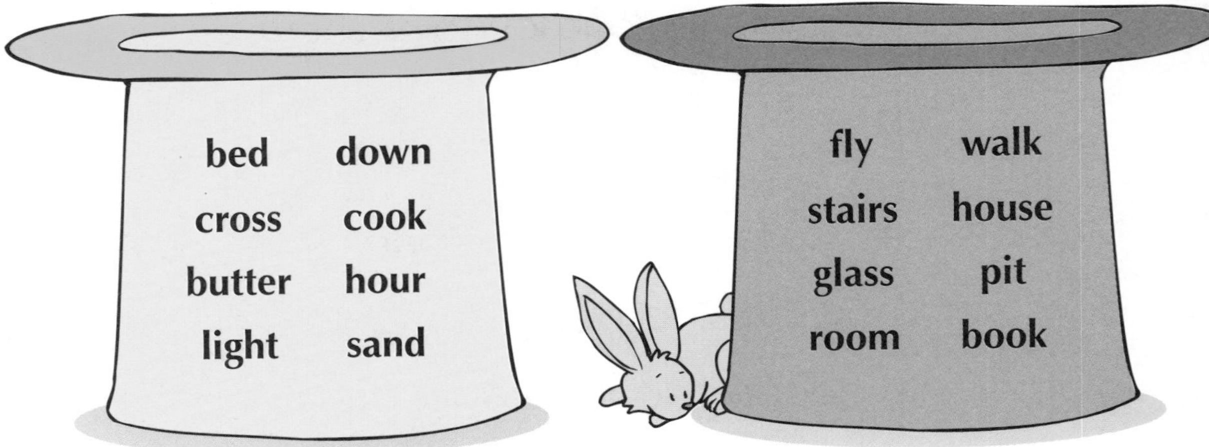

bed
down
cross
cook
butter
hour
light
sand
fly
walk
stairs
house
glass
pit
room
book

1. ____________ 2. ____________ 3. ____________

4. ____________ 5. ____________ 6. ____________

7. ____________ 8. ____________

Week 1

ENGLISH

E. Add an adjective to describe each underlined noun.

1. A <u>magician</u> can fool the audience.

   ____

2. Marco made the <u>watch</u> disappear.

   ____

3. The <u>neighbours</u> gathered in the backyard.

   ____

4. The <u>girl</u> volunteered to help the magician.

   ____

5. Rosa hung a <u>sign</u> on the fence.

   ____

6. The <u>lemonade</u> and the <u>cookies</u> were delicious.

   ____

   ____

7. A <u>rabbit</u> came out from Marco's <u>hat</u>.

   ____

   ____

8. Marco put on a <u>performance</u>.

   ____

   ____

A. Who eats who? For each of the following, copy each organism's name in its proper spot in the food chain.

Organism Pod 1 : bird, cat, leaf, beetle, spider

Producer → Consumer → Consumer

________ → ________ → ________

Organism Pod 2 : grasshopper, hawk, snake, clover, frog

Producer → Consumer → Consumer

________ → ________ → ________

Organism Pod 3 : osprey, plankton, water insect, large mouth bass, minnow

Producer → Consumer → Consumer

________ → ________ → ________

B. Complete the crossword puzzle by choosing the words from the Eco-bank.

Across

A. This one's supper? Only plants, please.
B. a word meaning "meat eater"
C. This is a word to describe all the non-living and living things together.
D. Using the sun, this organism makes its own food from non-living things.

Down

1. a living thing eating other living things
2. a name for the one that's being hunted
3. plant or animal eater
4. Hunter Alert! Watch out for this one...

Week 1

SCIENCE

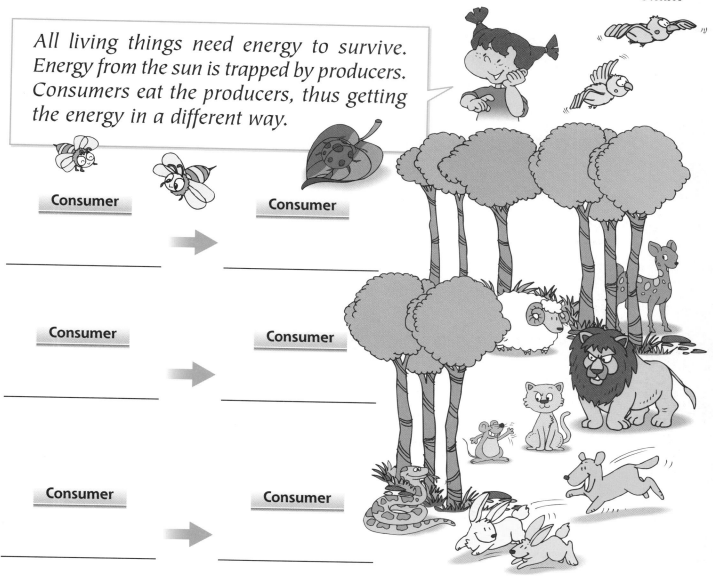

All living things need energy to survive. Energy from the sun is trapped by producers. Consumers eat the producers, thus getting the energy in a different way.

Consumer → Consumer
______ ______

Consumer → Consumer
______ ______

Consumer → Consumer
______ ______

Eco-bank

HERBIVORE
OMNIVORE
CARNIVORE
PREY
CONSUMER
PRODUCER
PREDATOR
ECOSYSTEM

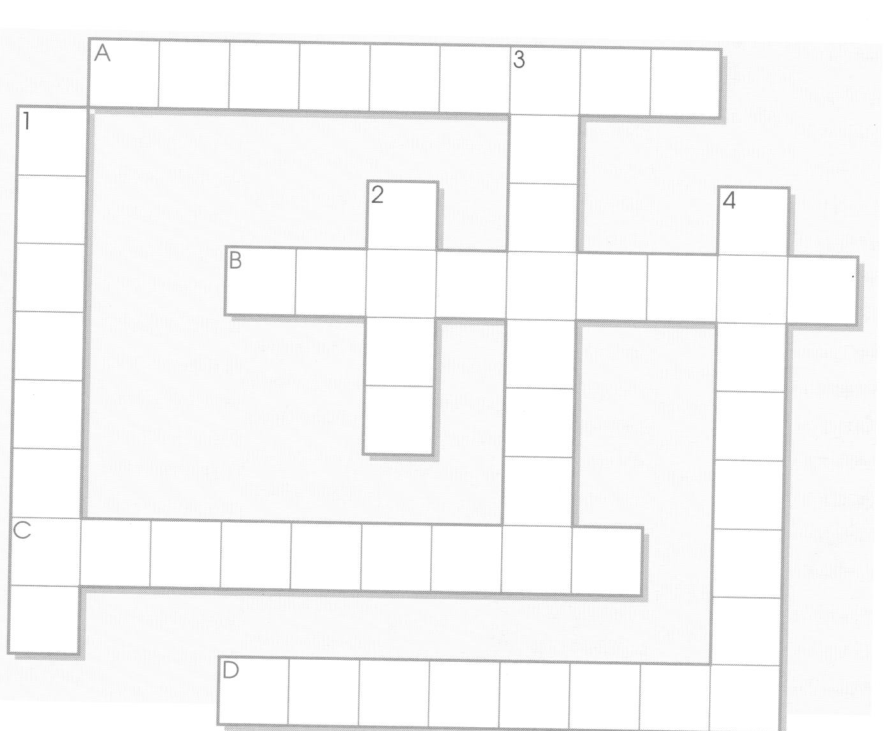

A. Label the map showing where the Aboriginal groups lived in Upper Canada.

Before the early settlers arrived in Upper Canada, there were already many Aboriginal peoples living there.

1. ____________

2. ____________

3. ____________

4. ____________

5. ____________

6. ____________

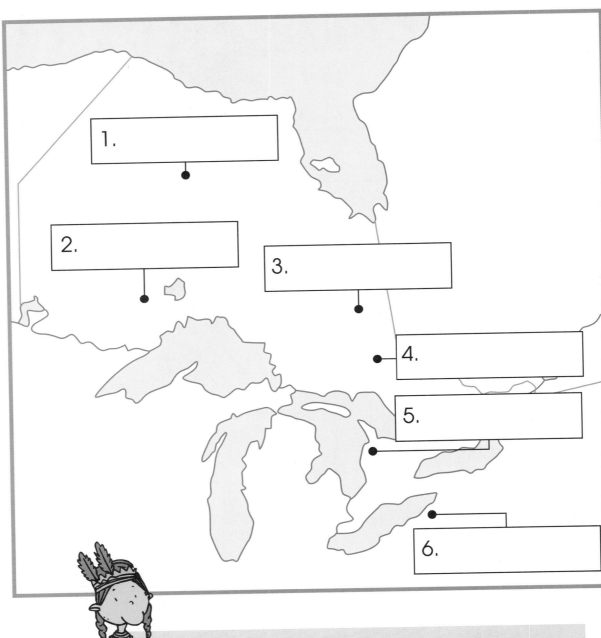

Algonquin Wendat Iroquois
Cree Ojibway Innu

B. Circle the things made by the Aboriginal peoples.

C. Read the statements about the Aboriginal peoples. Check ✔ the correct statements.

1. The Aboriginal peoples knew how to get syrup from maple trees. ☐
2. The early settlers learned a lot about farming from the Aboriginal peoples. ☐
3. In winter, the Aboriginal peoples stopped going outdoors. ☐
4. The Aboriginal peoples hunted animals for food and fur. ☐
5. They traded fur with the early settlers. ☐
6. On land, the Aboriginal peoples travelled on horse-drawn carriages. ☐

Week

1

ARTS & CRAFTS

HALLOWEEN FUN

Spooky Spider

Materials:

- 4 large black pipe cleaners
- 2 large googly eyes
- green yarn or string
- large black pompom
- glue

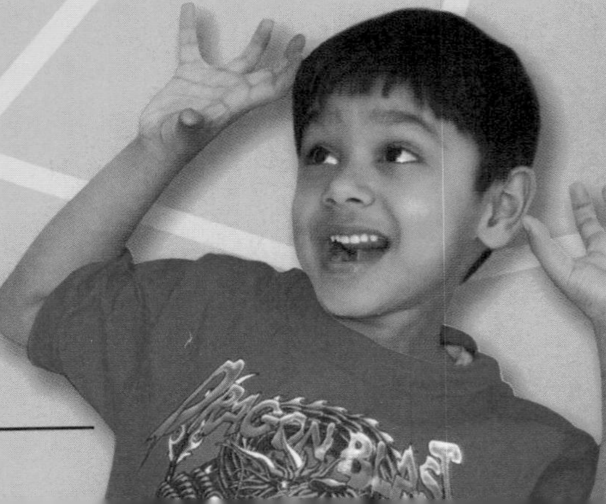

Directions:

1. Twist 2 pipe cleaners together at their centres.
2. Twist 1 more pipe cleaner and then the fourth until it looks like a spider.
3. Glue black pompom on top of spider.
4. Glue googly eyes onto pompom.
5. Add green string or yarn for hanging.

A. **Read the clues. Help Leon fill in the missing information on the brochure about Monster Park. Then answer the questions.**

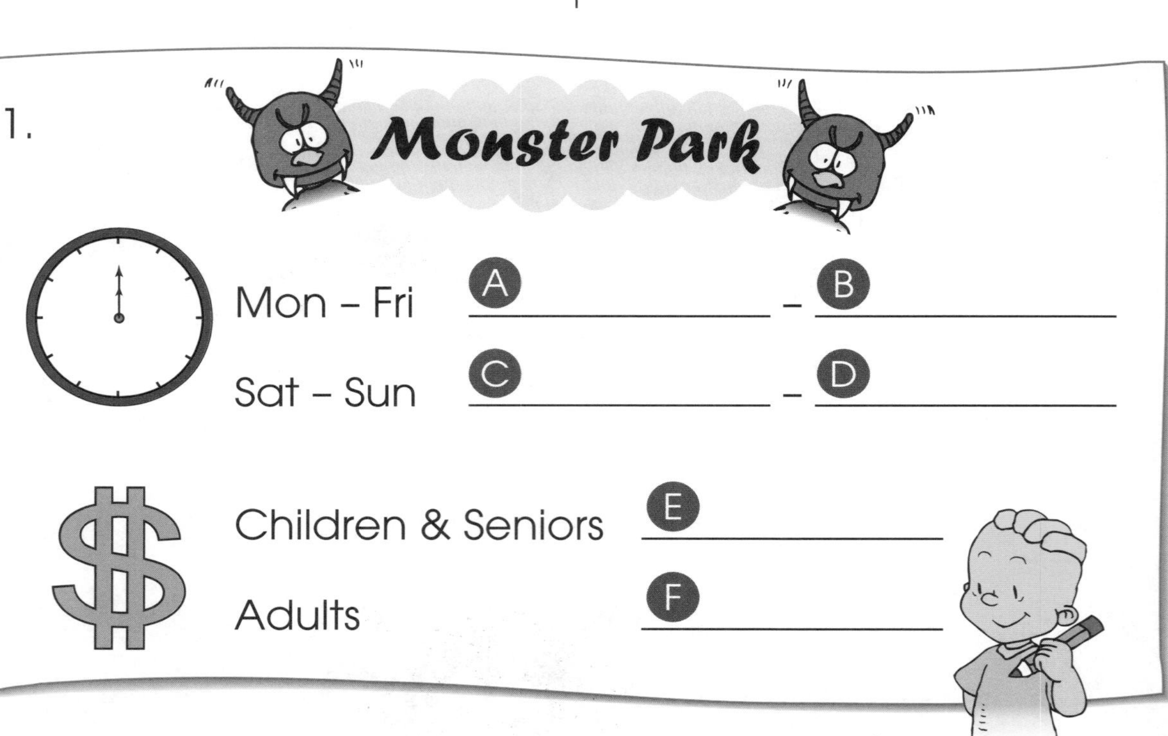

2. How long does the Park stay open on Wednesday? ________

3. How long does the Park stay open on Sunday? ________

4. If my parents take me to the Park, what are our admission fees? ________

Week 2

MATHEMATICS

B. Find how much money Leon and his parents have. Help each of them trade a bill of the greatest value with the money they have. Check ✓ the correct letter.

1.

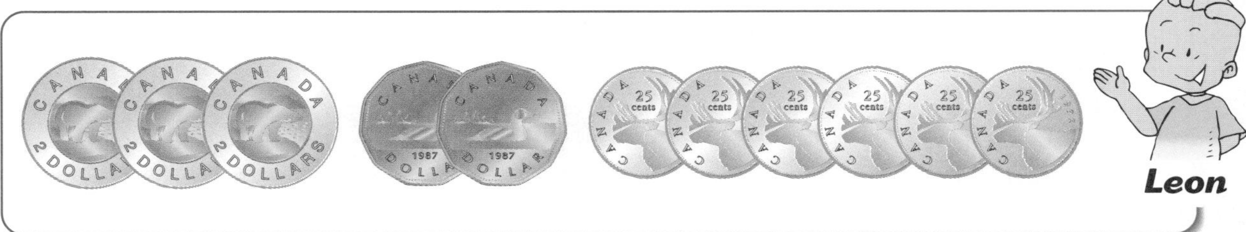

Leon has ______ dollars ______ cents or $ ______ .

He can trade a

A 
B 
C 
.

2.

Leon's dad has ______ dollars ______ cents or $ ______ .

He can trade a

A 
B 
C 
.

3.

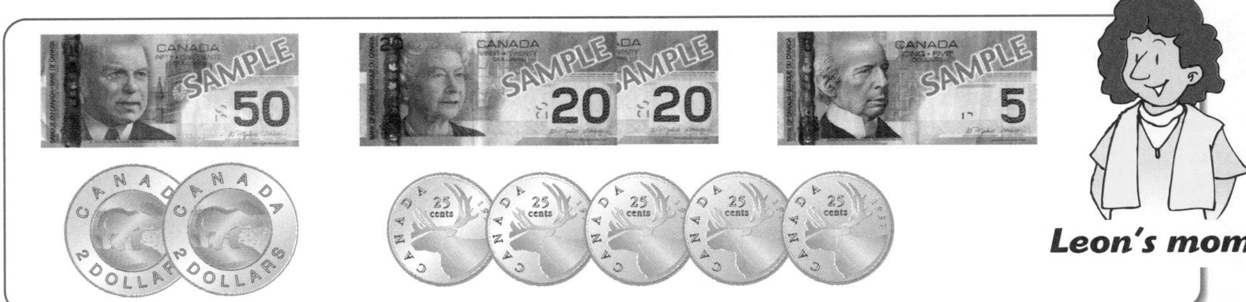

Leon's mom has ______ dollars ______ cents or $ ______ .

She can trade a

A 
B 
C 
.

C. **See what rides Leon's friends want to go on. Help them solve the problems.**

Ride Prices

Haunted Castle	$2.28	**Fright Coaster**	$3.15
Monster Pit	$1.98	**Blood Bath**	$2.59
Scary Mountain	$4.45		

*** $1.19 off for buying 3 or more tickets at the same time**

1. Lynda wants to go on "Scary Mountain" and "Fright Coaster". How much does she need to pay for the rides?

   She needs to pay $ ________ in all.

2. Timothy pays for a ride on "Haunted Castle" and one on "Blood Bath" with a $10 bill. How much change will he get?

   He will get $ ________ change.

3. John goes on "Monster Pit" with his parents. How much do they need to pay for the ride?

   They need to pay $ ________ .

D. See how many people are lining up for each ride. Help Leon fill in the blanks.

Haunted Castle

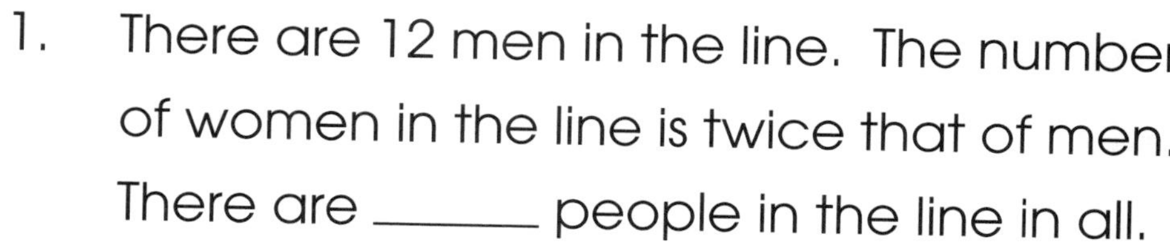

1. There are 12 men in the line. The number of women in the line is twice that of men. There are ______ people in the line in all.

Fright Coaster

2. There are 32 women, 45 men, 36 girls, and 28 boys in the line. There are ______ people in the line in all.

Monster Pit

3. There are 46 girls and 68 boys in the line. If 12 boys leave the line, there will be ______ people.

Blood Bath

4. $\frac{1}{2}$ of the people in the line are men. If 16 men are in the line, there are ______ people in the line in all.

Solve the problem.

Leon is in the line for "Scary Mountain". There are 47 boys in front of him and 28 girls behind him. How many boys have to leave the line in order to have 15 more boys than girls?

______ boys

The Robert Munsch Collection

Mud Puddle, Love You Forever, and *The Paper Bag Princess* have one thing in common. They are all books written by the famous author, Robert Munsch.

Robert Munsch was born on June 11, 1945 in Pittsburgh, Pennsylvania. He grew up in a family of nine kids. Munsch, surprisingly, did not do well as a student but he did write poetry during his years at school. In high school, he did not have many friends so he spent his time reading books.

After high school, Robert Munsch studied for seven years to be a priest and worked part-time at an orphanage. It was then that he realized that he was no longer interested in becoming a priest; instead he enjoyed working with children. He got a job in a daycare. There, he told a story to a group of children. The story was called "Mortimer". 12 years later, *Mortimer* became a book.

Robert Munsch and his wife then moved to Canada. His boss at a preschool encouraged him to publish his stories. He took two months off and wrote ten stories that he sent to ten publishers. Nine publishers rejected his works but one agreed to publish a story called "Mud Puddle". Since the publication of *Mud Puddle*, Robert Munsch has written 35 more books. Today, he continues to write stories that bring smiles to the faces of both children and adults throughout the world.

A. Write "T" for the true sentences and "F" for the false ones.

1. ______ Robert Munsch is a famous author.
2. ______ He was very popular at school.
3. ______ Robert Munsch was a priest.
4. ______ He began telling stories to children in a daycare.
5. ______ *Mud Puddle* was his first published book.

The first word and all important words in a book title begin with a capital letter. Book titles are sometimes underlined when they are written.

B. Rewrite each sentence using proper capitalization.

1. mud puddle was the first book that Robert Munsch had published.

____

____

2. Peter read his class a story called get out of bed.

____

3. charlotte's web is a novel about a friendship between a pig and a spider.

____

____

4. love you forever became a bestseller in Canada.

Love You Forever

____

____

C. **Read the clues and complete the crossword puzzle with words from the passage.**

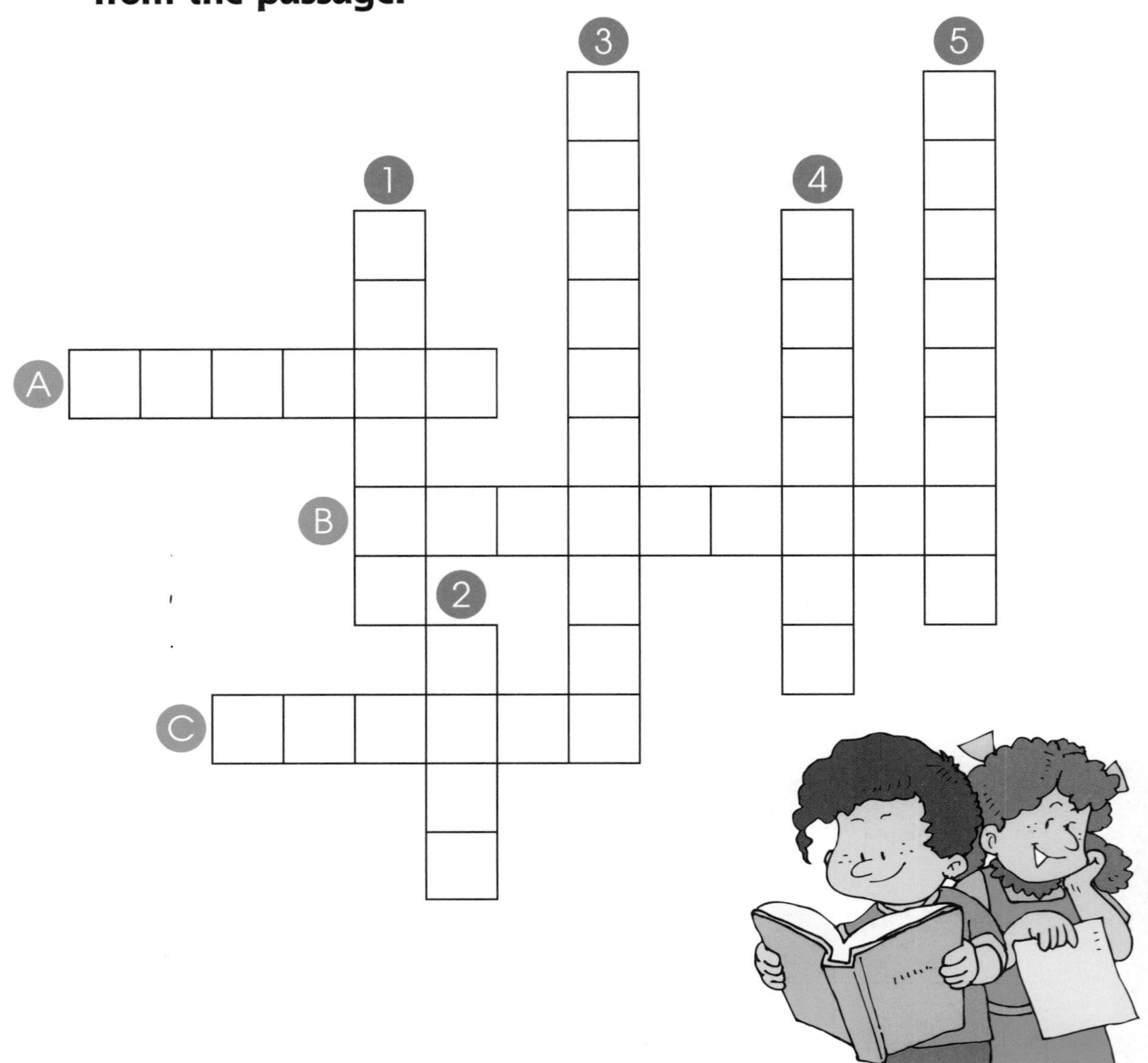

Across

A. grown-ups

B. where children without parents are taken care of

C. well-known

Down

1. writer

2. superior

3. companies that publish books

4. where young children are taken care of

5. refused to accept

D. Robert Munsch has written many books. Place the following book titles in alphabetical order.

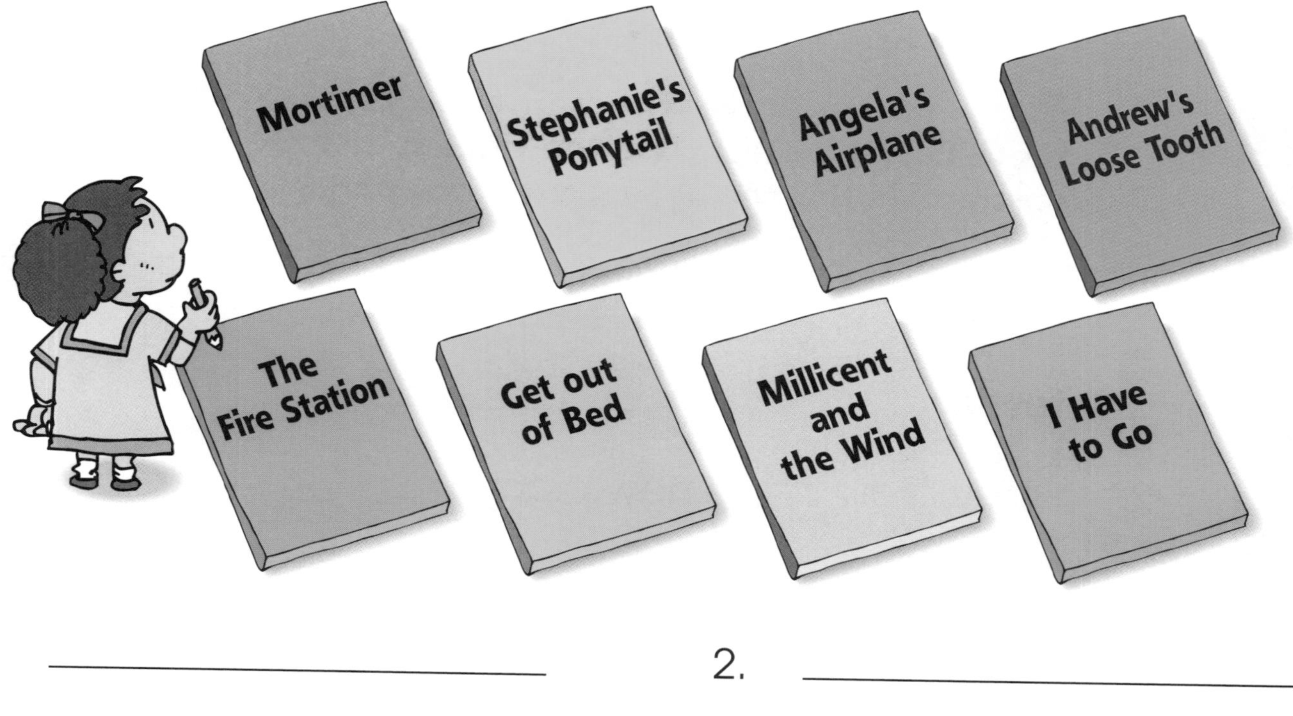

1. ____________________ 2. ____________________

3. ____________________ 4. ____________________

5. ____________________ 6. ____________________

7. ____________________ 8. ____________________

E. Robert Munsch is coming to speak to your class. Write five questions that you would like to ask him.

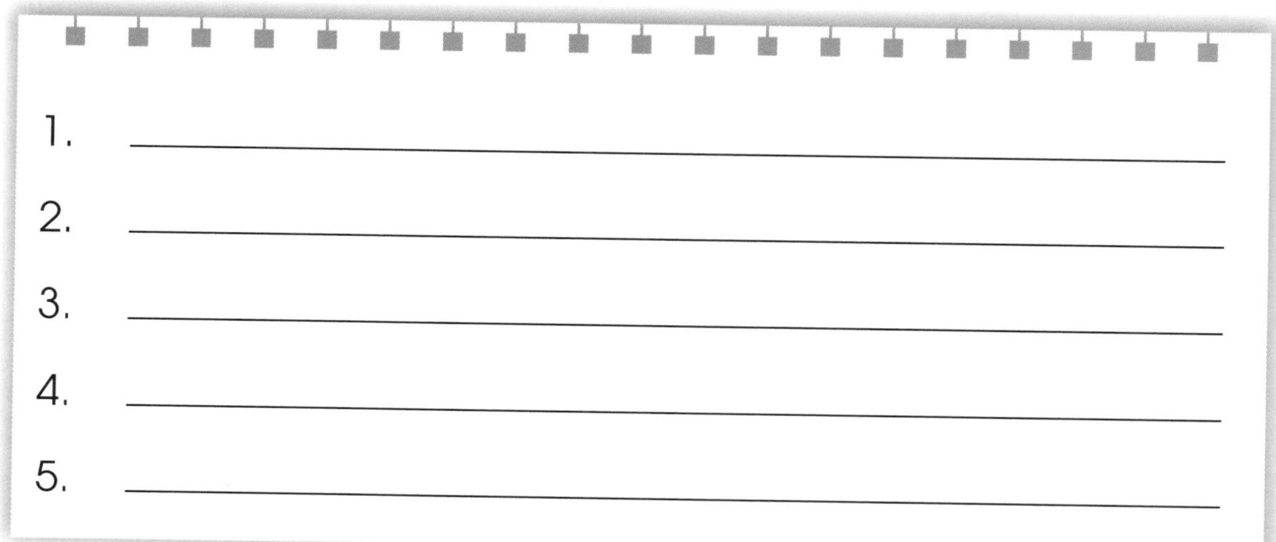

1. ____________________
2. ____________________
3. ____________________
4. ____________________
5. ____________________

A. Many plants have the same parts as these flower plants. Use the clues to help unscramble the names of these plant parts.

1. I am often colourful and nice smelling. I may produce seeds.

   fewlor ____________________

2. I may grow into a new plant.

   edes ____________________

3. I am usually green, and I use the sun and water to make food for the plant.

   efal ____________________

4. I am like a straw. Water travels through me to reach the leaves.

   tmes ____________________

5. We gather water and nutrients from the soil, and we hold the plant in place.

   storo ____________________

B. Try this!

To prove that water travels up the stem and to the leaves, try putting a celery stick in a glass of water with a few drops of blue food colour. Use celery with some leaves still attached. Let it sit in the water overnight.

Week 2 SCIENCE

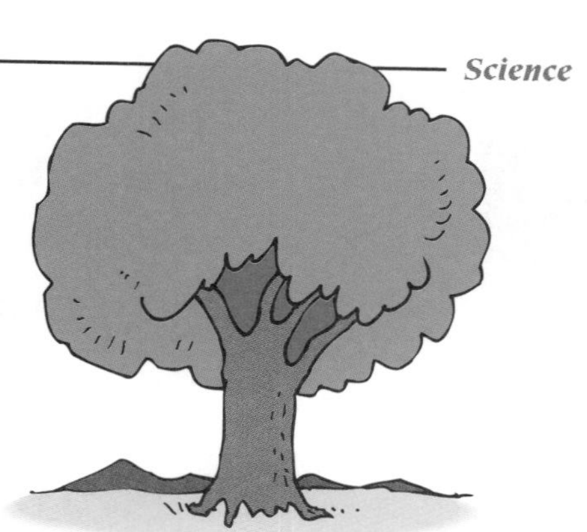

C. Pick the word from the word bank that correctly completes each sentence.

water	trunk	plants	nutrients
branches	bark	leaves	

Trees are the largest 1.____________ . Instead of a stem, trees have a 2.____________ . Like a stem, it delivers 3.____________ and 4.____________ to the 5.____________ of the tree. It also supports the 6.____________ . This part of the tree is protected by a special skin called 7.____________ .

D. Fill in the blanks with the given words.

light water nutrients air energy

Plants get 1.____________ from the sun.

Leaves need 2.____________ , 3.____________ , and 4.____________ to make food.

Plants get 5.____________ from the soil.

Week 2

SOCIAL STUDIES

A. **Read what the early settlers in Upper Canada say. Check ✓ the correct statements and cross ✗ the wrong ones.**

1. *The journey across the ocean was long and tiring.*
2. *I hope to lead a better life here.*
3. *There are more job opportunities here than in Germany.*
4. *Education is better here.*
5. *I don't like the government in my home country.*
6. *I enjoy touring around the world.*
7. *We came here by railway.*

B. Label the map showing the places of origin and the routes of the early settlers.

St. Lawrence River	Scotland	England
Germany	Atlantic Ocean	Italy

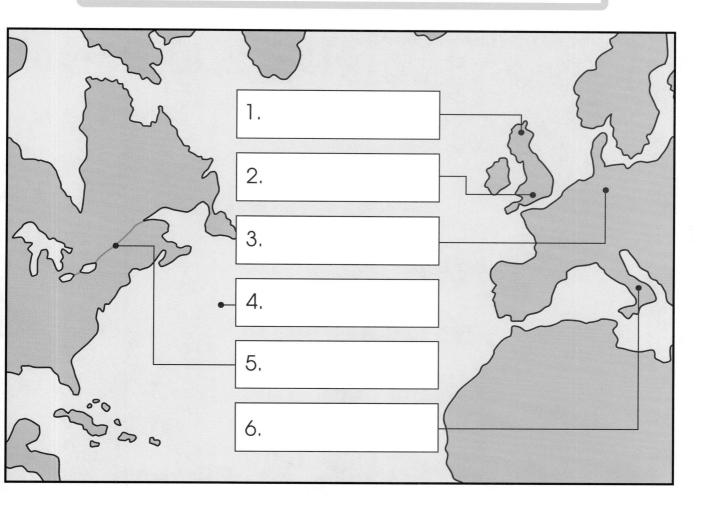

1.
2.
3.
4.
5.
6.

In 1800, there were about 35 000 people in Upper Canada.

Week

2

ARTS & CRAFTS

Flower Power

Materials:

- popsicle sticks
- construction paper of different colours
- paint
- glue
- yogurt cup
- scissors
- wrapping paper
- brown tissue paper

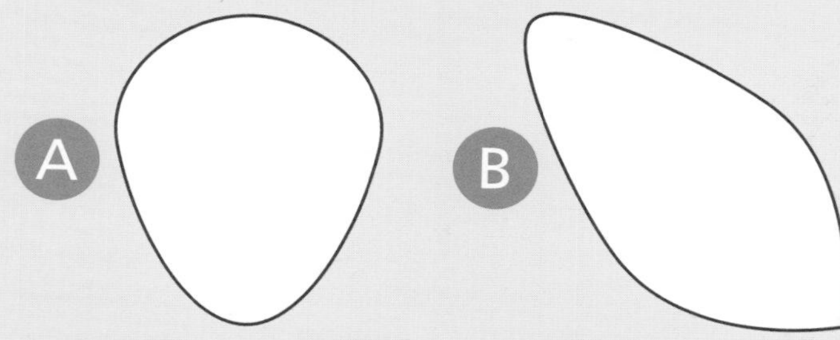

Directions:

1. Using tracer A, trace 5 petals per flower to desired number of flowers.
2. Cut circles (centres) for flowers.
3. Glue petals to centres.
4. Paint popsicle sticks. Let dry.
5. Trace leaves B and glue to "stem".
6. Glue "flower" to "stem" with leaves.
7. Wrap yogurt cup with wrapping paper.
8. Fill pot with brown tissue paper.
9. "Plant" flowers.

A. See how Aunt Daisy puts her groceries. Help her solve the problems.

1. 15 cans ; 3 shelves

   ______ cans on each shelf

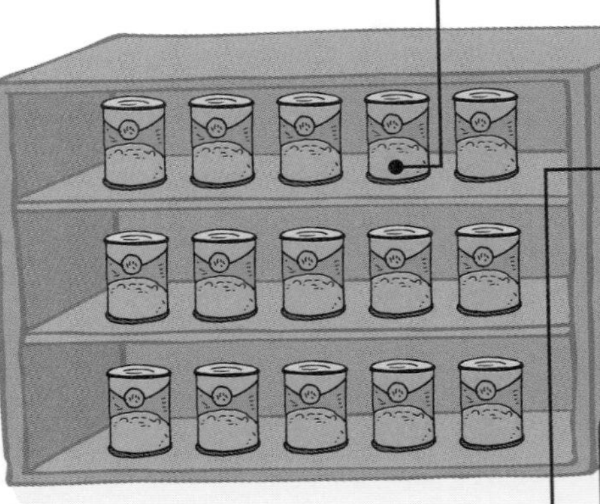

2. 16 hot dog buns ; 2 bags

   ______ hot dog buns in each bag

3. 24 cookies ; 3 trays

   ______ cookies on each tray

4. 20 cans ; 4 piles

   ______ cans in each pile

5. 21 boxes ; 7 packs

   ______ boxes in each pack

Week 3

MATHEMATICS

B. See how much Aunt Daisy pays for her groceries. Help her record the cost of each item and find the change.

1.

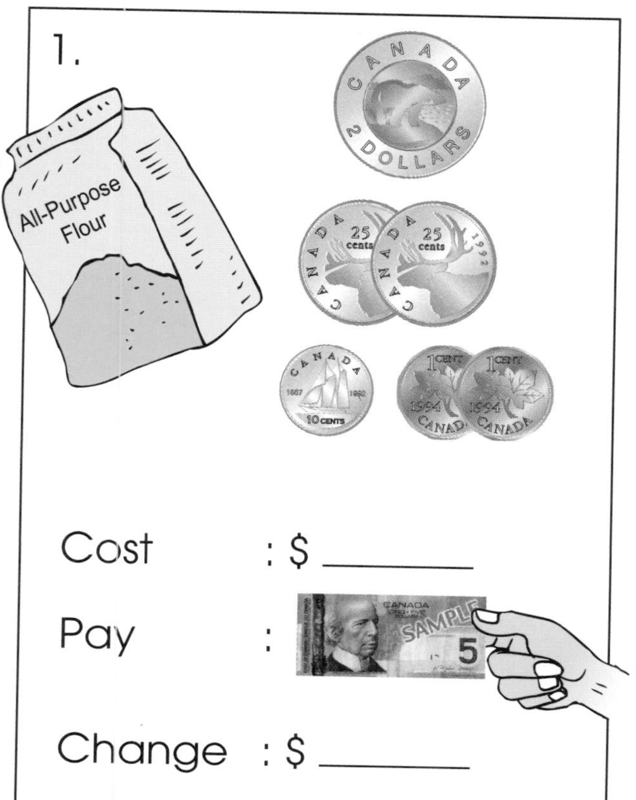

Cost : $ ________

Pay :

Change : $ ________

2.

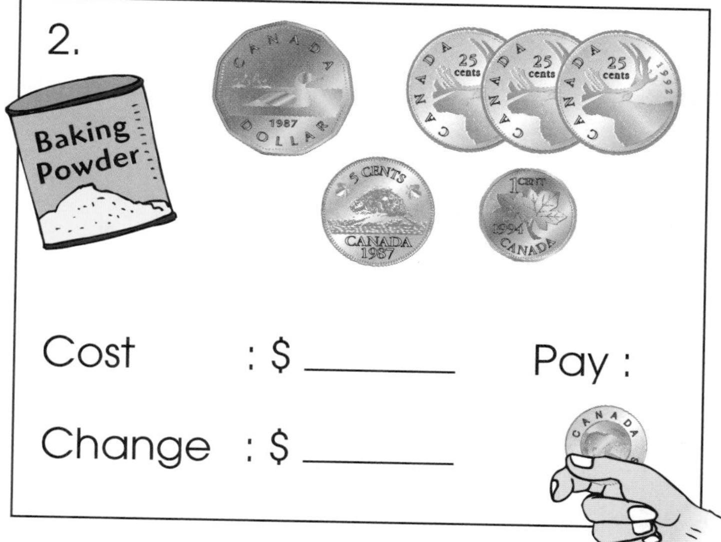

Cost : $ ________

Pay :

Change : $ ________

3.

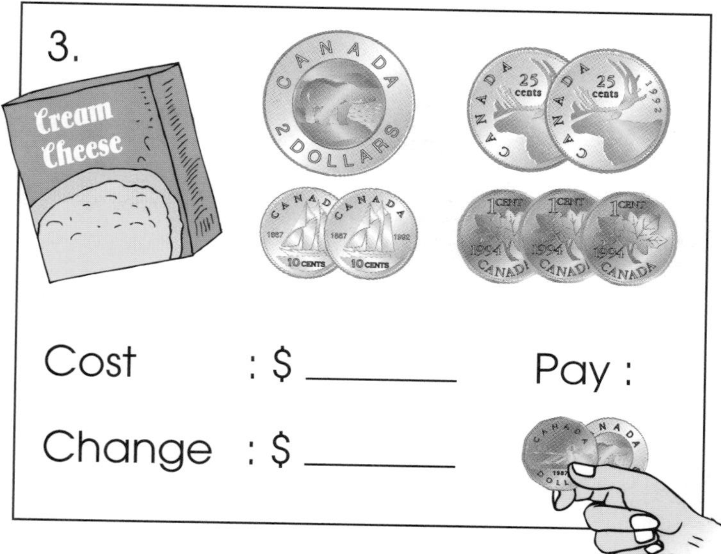

Cost : $ ________

Pay :

Change : $ ________

4.

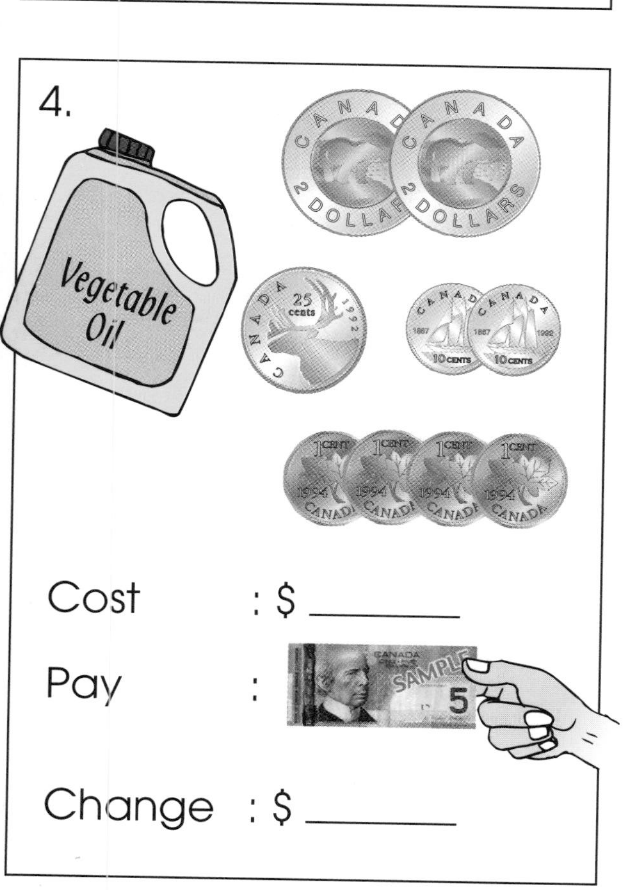

Cost : $ ________

Pay :

Change : $ ________

5.

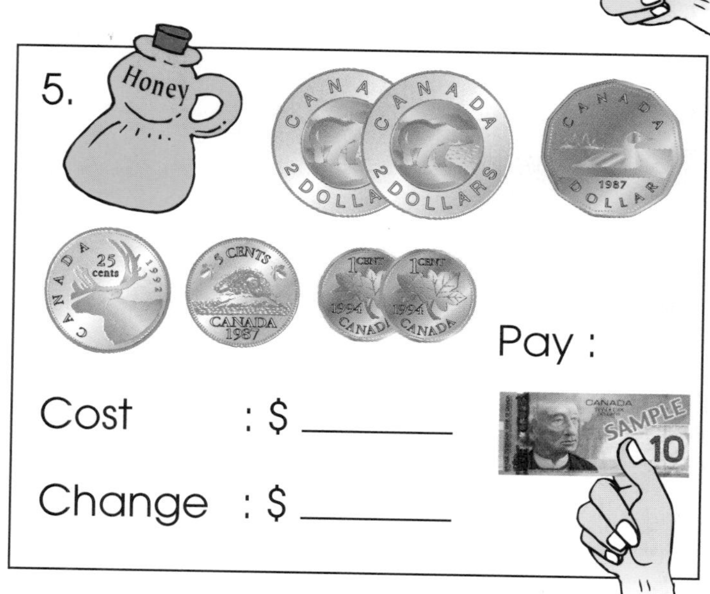

Pay :

Cost : $ ________

Change : $ ________

C. **Help Aunt Daisy record the baking time and temperature for each goodie.**

1.

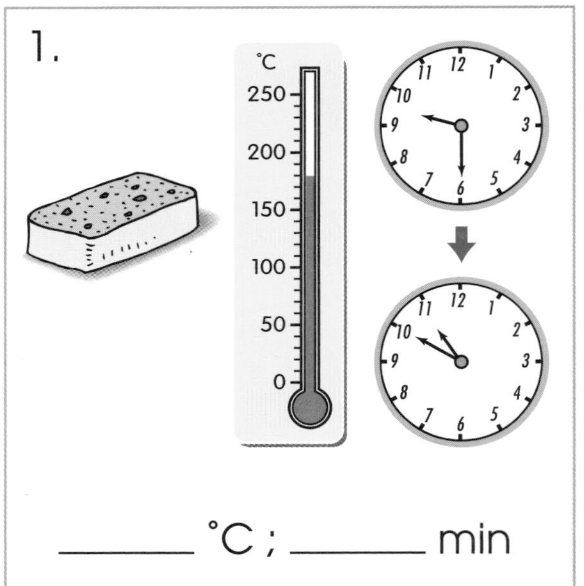

______ °C ; ______ min

2.

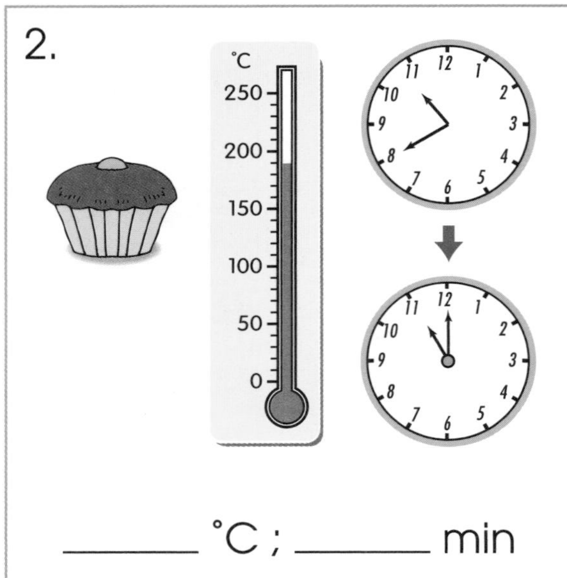

______ °C ; ______ min

3.

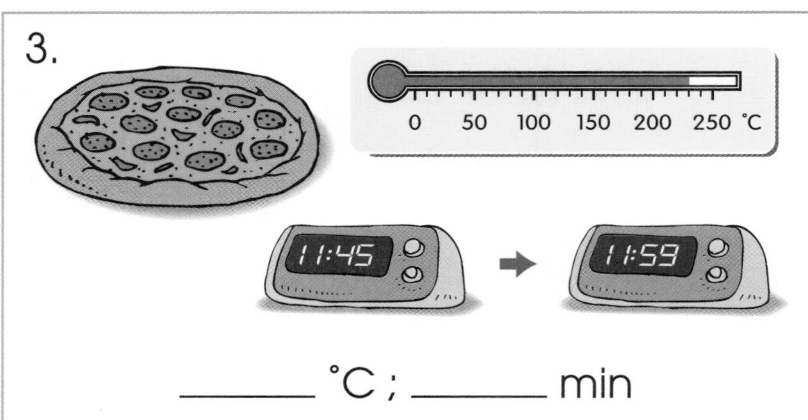

______ °C ; ______ min

4.

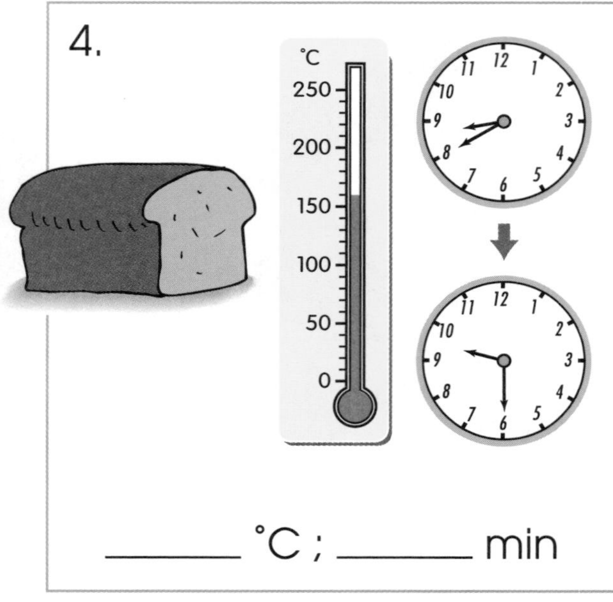

______ °C ; ______ min

5.

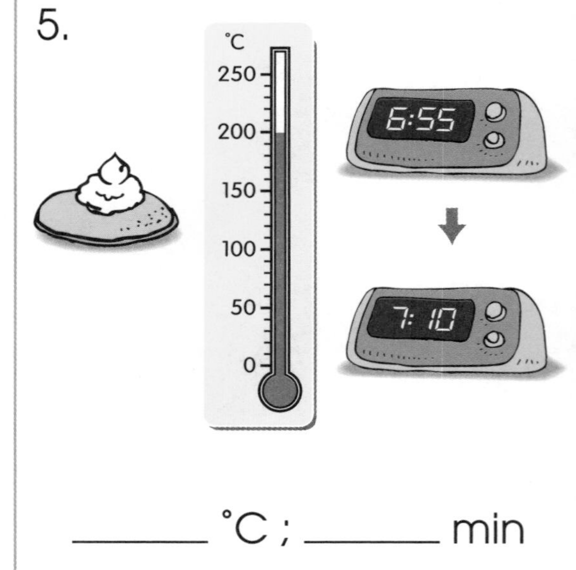

______ °C ; ______ min

Week 3

MATHEMATICS

D. Aunt Daisy got some raffle tickets from buying groceries. Help her draw shapes to complete the patterns and do the skill questions. Then measure and find the perimeter of each ticket.

1.

295 + 639 = ______

Perimeter = ______ cm

2.

7 x 7 = ______

Perimeter = ______ cm

3.

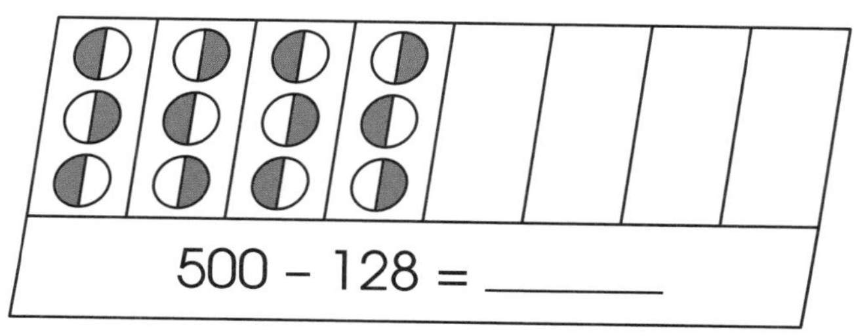

Perimeter = ______ cm

Help Derek the Alien find a path to reach the spaceship. He can only pass through the correct multiplication sentences.

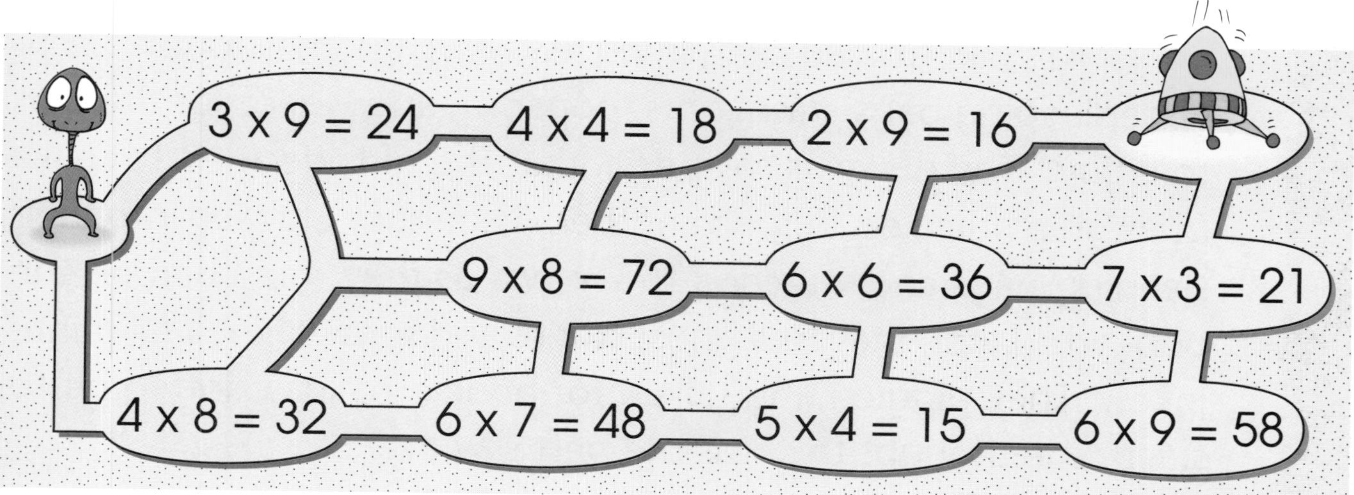

A Day with Friends

It was a hot August day. Julia invited her friends Vanessa and Nadia over for a pool party. While her mom supervised, the girls had swimming races and diving contests, and they even played volleyball in the pool. When they got tired, they stopped to float on the air mattress.

After swimming, Julia's mother invited Vanessa and Nadia to stay for dinner. They had hot dogs, chips, and fresh watermelon. The sun was beginning to set and Julia felt sad that her friends would have to go home soon. Julia's mother said she had a surprise for all of them. She had arranged for Vanessa and Nadia to stay overnight. The girls cheered with delight.

Julia's parents had everything ready in the family room. There were sleeping bags, flashlights, popcorn, and videos for the girls to enjoy. The day was so special that the girls decided to make friendship bracelets for one another. Then they crawled into their sleeping bags and watched the movie as they munched on the popcorn. Later, they told ghost stories and some of their favourite jokes. They giggled and talked for hours. As Julia drifted off to sleep, she thought this was the best day ever.

A. In each box, draw one thing that the girls did on this fun day and write a caption to explain what was happening.

____________________	____________________
____________________	____________________

B. Add your own ideas to the following lists.

Characteristic of a Good Friend	Recipe Word	Measurement
1. kindness	1. add	1. cup
2. trust	2. mix	2. teaspoon
3. ________	3. ________	3. ________
4. ________	4. ________	4. ________
5. ________	5. ________	5. ________

C. **Using words from the lists in (B), create a recipe for what it takes to be a good friend. Look at some recipes to help you gather ideas.**

A Recipe for Being a

Good Friend

- Add 1 cup of kindness.

D. **Make a list of all your friends. Connect the names by connecting common letters in the names.**

Example: JULIA
VANESSA
NADIA

```
        V
J U L I A
        N A D I A
        E
        S
        S
        A
```

My friends

E. Follow the example. Write what they probably said.

Example: **Julia invited her friends Vanessa and Nadia over for a pool party.**

Julia said to Vanessa and Nadia, "Would you like to come over for a pool party?"

1. Julia's mother invited Vanessa and Nadia to stay for dinner.

2. Julia's mother said she had a surprise for all of them.

3. Julia suggested making friendship bracelets for one another.

4. Julia asked her mother if they could have pizza for dinner.

5. Julia told her mother that it was the best day ever.

Plant Pollination and **Seed** Dispersion

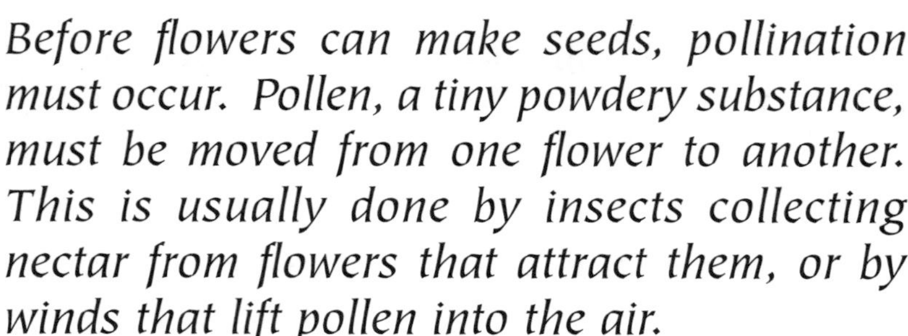

Before flowers can make seeds, pollination must occur. Pollen, a tiny powdery substance, must be moved from one flower to another. This is usually done by insects collecting nectar from flowers that attract them, or by winds that lift pollen into the air.

A. Choose the correct ending for each of these verses.

Ⓐ the sea
Ⓑ a bee
Ⓒ your knee

Pretty to smell
Pretty to see
From flower to flower
By way of 1. ______

Ⓐ some keys
Ⓑ some cheese
Ⓒ a breeze

Drifting through air
I may make you sneeze
From flower to flower
By way of 2. ______

B. For each of these plants, determine whether they are "wind pollinated" or "insect pollinated". Write the letters.

Wind pollinated

Insect pollinated

C. Match each picture with the description of seed dispersal.

A. Eaten by animal, seed passes as waste in a different place.

B. Fall from plant, "wings" take seed further from plant.

C. Float along ocean currents to sprout at a distant shore.

D. Parachute a distance through the air.

E. Buried and forgotten by an animal.

F. Hitch a ride with an animal that brushes by the plant.

Science Fun

Some plants are pollinated by flies. To attract the flies to them, they smell like rotting meat!

D. Try this!

Put on a pair of old socks over your shoes and go for a walk along a planted area. If there are any hitch-hiking seeds, your socks should pick them up.

A. Circle the correct answer for each statement about corn.

The Aboriginal peoples taught us how to grow corn.

1. The Aboriginal peoples taught the early settlers to fertilize the soil with _____ .

   A. water B. fish C. dung

2. The dried kernels were ground into flour called _____ .

   A. cornmeal B. cornflakes C. dough

3. The flour from corn was used to make _____ .

   A. chips B. pizza C. bread

4. The early settlers also grew _____ under corn stalks.

   A. peppers B. beans C. strawberries

5. Bannock was a kind of _____ made from corn.

   A. bread B. pudding C. porridge

6. Dried corn was also used for _____ .

   A. decoration B. feeding animals

   C. making snacks

Challenge

We have a snack made by heating kernels. Do you know what it is?

____

B. Trees provided a lot of useful things for the settlers. Complete the statements with the words from the word bank.

maple bark poplar
birch canoes syrup
tea tonic

1. The ____________ of spruce was used to make ____________ .

2. The sap from ____________ trees could be made into ____________ .

3. The inner bark of ____________ trees was useful as a healthy ____________ .

4. ____________ bark was used to make ____________ .

C. Cross out ✗ the wooden things we rarely make or use today.

1.	log cabins	☐	2.	pails	☐
3.	farming tools	☐	4.	rolling pins	☐
5.	fences	☐	6.	toys	☐
7.	bowls	☐	8.	furniture	☐
9.	canoes	☐	10.	pitch forks	☐

Cosmic Mobile

Week 3

ARTS & CRAFTS

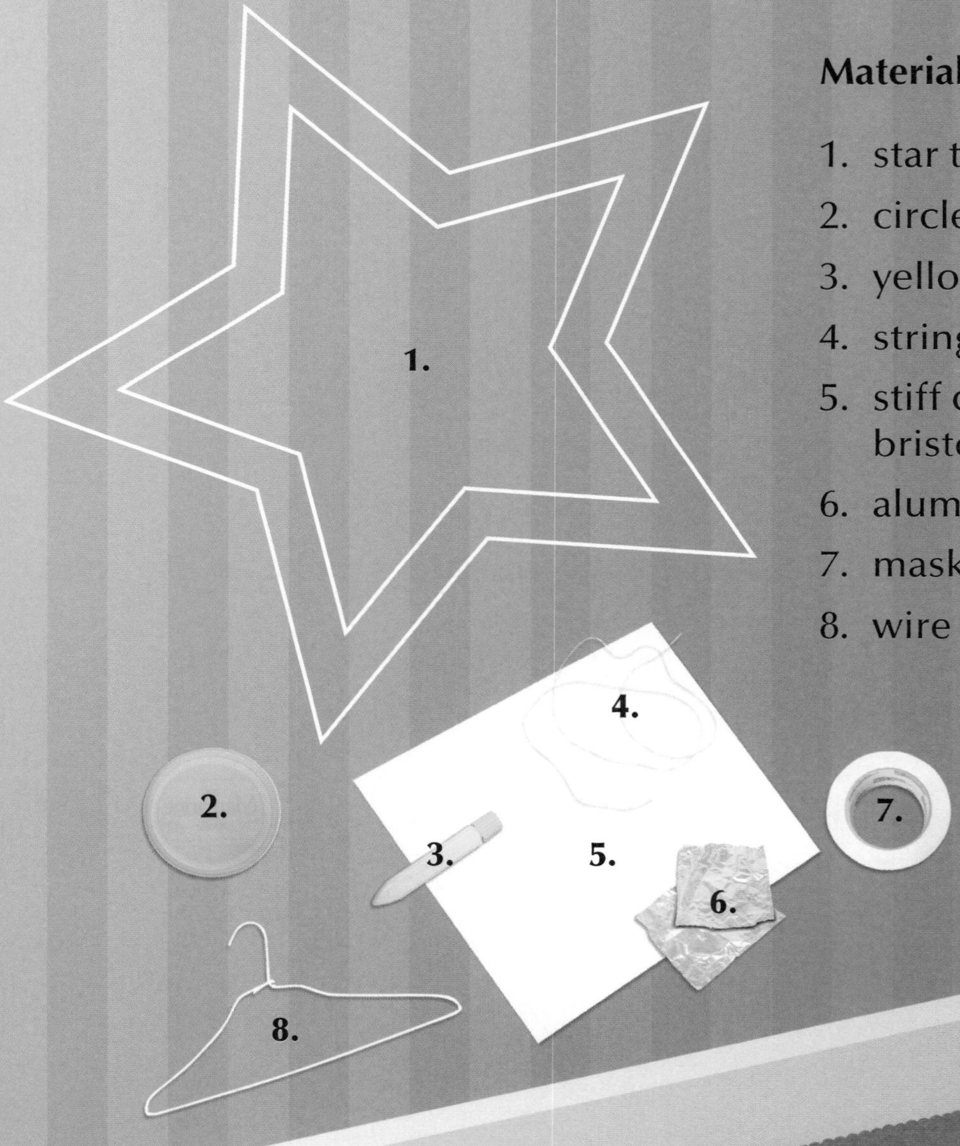

1.

Materials:

1. star tracers
2. circle tracers
3. yellow paint
4. string
5. stiff cardboard or bristol board
6. aluminum foil
7. masking tape
8. wire hanger

4. 2. 3. 5. 7. 6. 8.

Directions:

1. Pull wire hanger into circular shape.
2. Using star and circle tracers, trace stars and circles on bristol board or cardboard.
3. Cut some of the large circles into quarter moons and half moons.
4. Cover stars with foil.
5. Paint moons yellow. Let dry.
6. Attach moons and stars to wire hanger with string.

A. **Ellen and her friends have drawn some shapes. Look at their shapes and draw lines to help them divide the shapes. Then write fractions to complete the sentences.**

1. 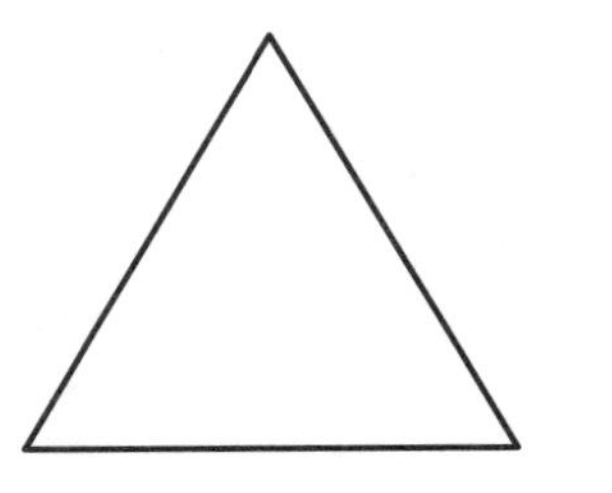

Ellen

Divide the shape into 3 equal parts. Colour 1 part. ______ of the shape is coloured.

2. 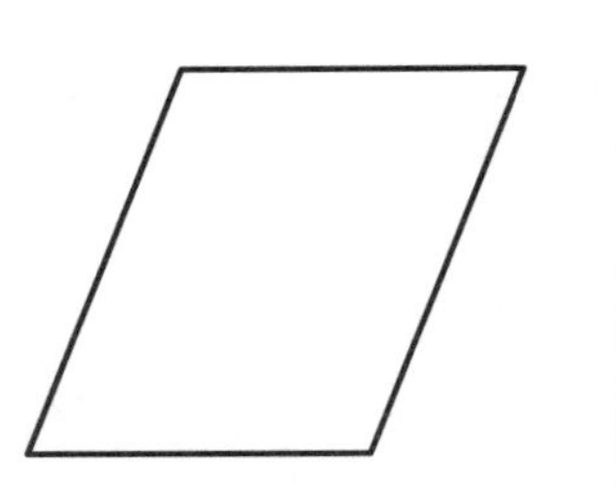

John

Divide the shape into 4 equal parts. Colour 2 parts. ______ of the shape is coloured.

3. 

Patrick

Divide the shape into 8 equal parts. Colour 5 parts. ______ of the shape is coloured.

4. 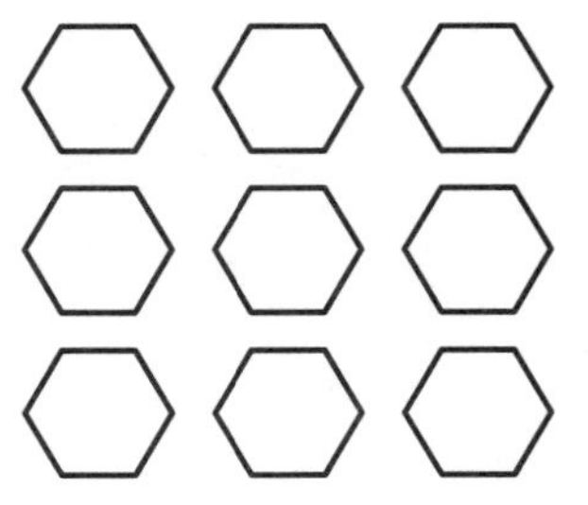

Ivy

Divide the shapes into 3 groups. Colour 2 groups. ______ of the shapes are coloured.

5. 

Tiffany

Divide the shapes into 3 groups. Colour 2 groups. ______ of the shapes are coloured.

B. Look at the children's shapes again. Help them complete the table.

	Children	Name of Shape	Number of Sides	Number of Vertices
1.	Ellen			
2.	John			
3.	Patrick			
4.	Ivy			
5.	Tiffany			

C. The Art teacher, Mrs. Louis, drew some shapes on the board. Help the children identify the shapes. Colour the shapes that are congruent to the one on the left yellow and the shapes that are similar red.

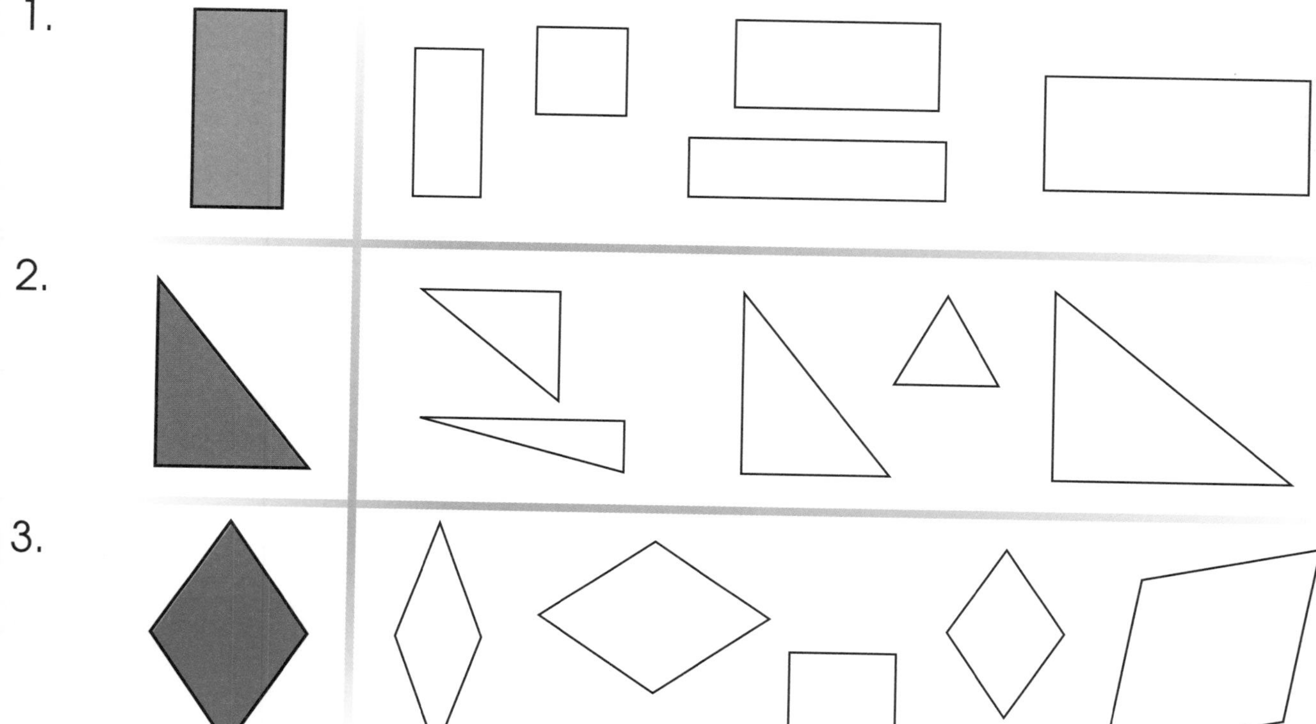

Week 4

MATHEMATICS

D. Look at the children's scores for their drawings. Refer to the graph and answer the questions.

1. Who got the highest score? __________

2. What was the highest score? __________

3. Who got the lowest score? __________

4. What was the lowest score? __________

5. Who had 5 marks more than Ivy? __________

6. Who had 15 marks fewer than Ellen? __________

7. How many children had a mark below 65? __________

8. If the full mark is 100, how many more marks does Ivy need to get full mark? __________

E. Mrs. Louis gives each child a sticker. Look at the children's stickers. Help them draw the images for the stickers.

	Reflection Image	Translation Image	Rotation Image
1.			
2.			
3.			
4. B			
5.			

Sand Sand

Solve the problem.

Two packets of sand weigh 9 kg. If one packet is twice as heavy as the other, what is the weight of the heavier bag?

The weight of the heavier bag is ________ kg.

The Emperor Penguin is one of the largest members of the penguin family. It can weigh up to 30 kilograms and stand as high as 1.1 metres. Male and female Emperor Penguins look alike. They have black feathers, a light coloured belly, webbed black feet, and a black bill with a yellow-orange streak. They live in Antarctica which is located in the southern hemisphere.

A female Emperor Penguin lays only one egg. It then leaves to gather food while the male penguin keeps watch over the egg. The father has a special layer of feathered skin called the brood pouch that keeps the egg safe and warm. For 65 days the male does not eat anything as he stands and protects the egg from icy temperatures, harsh winds, and snowstorms.

Two months later, after the chick has hatched, the mother returns. She brings food and takes over protecting the newborn baby in her brood pouch. It continues to be an important job because if the chick falls out, it could freeze to death in two minutes. Within two months the chick is old enough to be left alone while its parents go out to find food. Eventually, the baby penguin is old enough to hunt for its own food.

Emperor Penguins have an interesting way of adapting to the cold environment. Their survival depends on teamwork. The penguins huddle together in a huge group. They take turns moving from the cold outer edge of the circle into the centre until they warm up and are ready to move back to the outside. The Emperor Penguin is certainly a peculiar but interesting bird.

A. Find out what is wrong with the following sentences. Correct the sentences and write them on the lines.

1. The Emperor Penguin has a yellow-orange bill with a black streak.

2. Emperor Penguins live in the North Pole.

3. The brood pouch keeps the father penguin safe and warm.

4. Chicks could freeze to death within an hour.

5. Baby penguins take a month or so to hatch.

6. The penguins huddle together in small groups.

B. Read the clues and complete the crossword puzzle with words from the passage.

Across

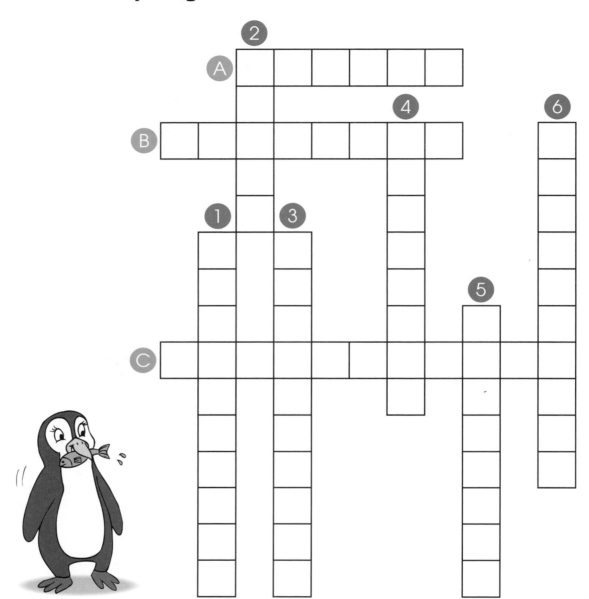

A. stand close together

B. continuing to live

C. the surroundings

Down

1. finally
2. rough, severe
3. one half of the Earth
4. changing
5. strange, odd
6. guarding, defending

C. Using facts about penguins, write an acrostic poem about this peculiar creature.

P ______________________________

 ______________________________

 ______________________________

 ______________________________

 ______________________________

 ______________________________

 ______________________________

 ______________________________

D. Use the grid to solve the riddle.

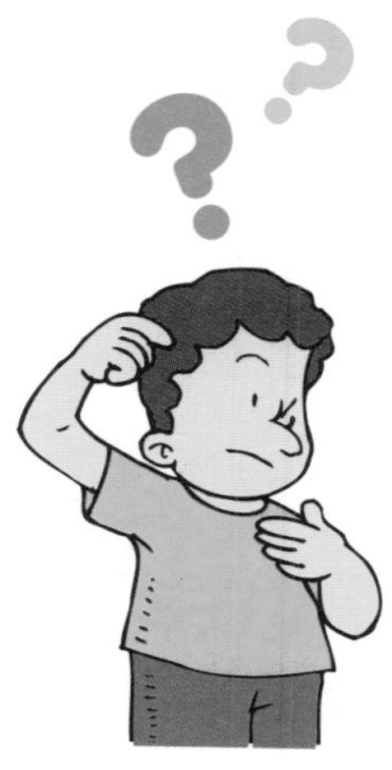

E	c	z	b	f	p
D	e	i	u	o	v
C	j	n	h	a	t
B	y	w	d	q	g
A	s	x	r	l	m
	1	**2**	**3**	**4**	**5**

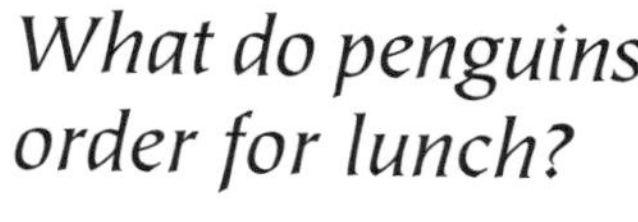
What do penguins
order for lunch?

___ ___ ___ ___ ___ ___ ___ ___ ___ ___

2D 1E 1D 3E 1D 3A 5B 1D 3A 1A

A. **Buddy hears a lot of noise. See how he scales the noise from the radio. Help him colour the bars to show the loudness of the noise from the things below.**

1. 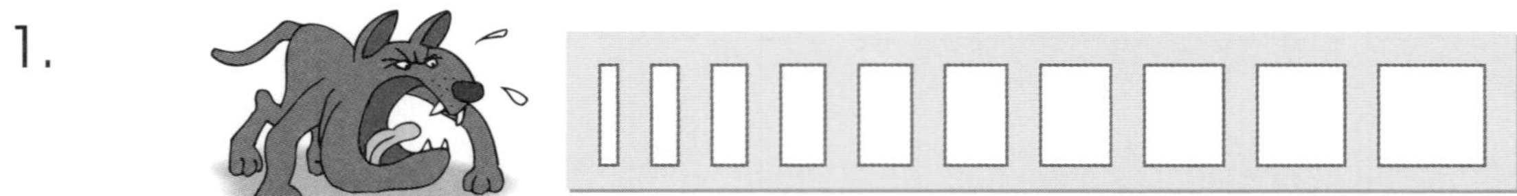

2. 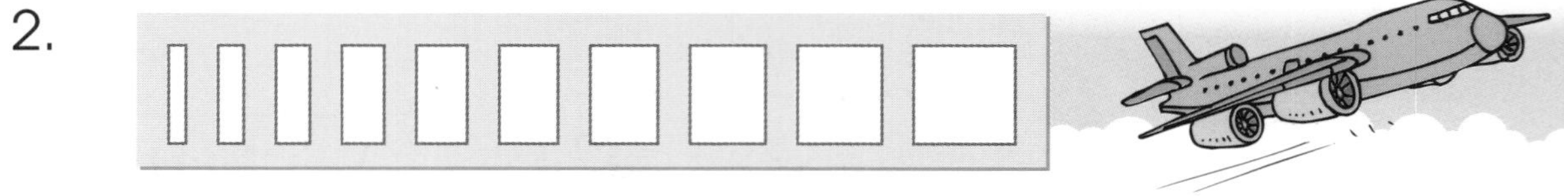

3. 

4. 

5. 

Week 4

SCIENCE

B. Write "N" for natural light and "A" for artificial light.

C. Take some time now to stop and listen. You will hear so many things. List the first five things you hear.

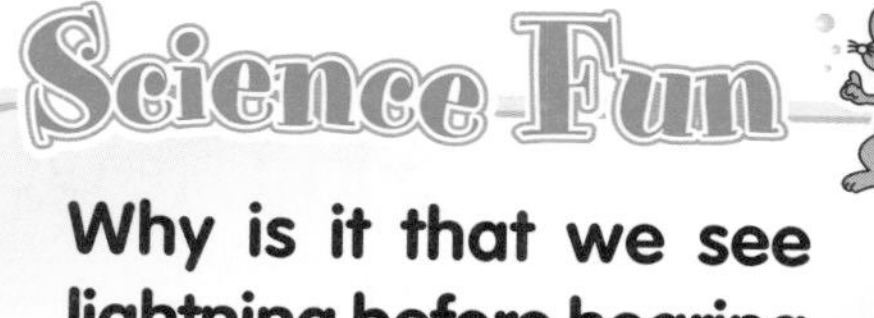

Why is it that we see lightning before hearing thunder?

1. ______________________________

2. ______________________________

3. ______________________________

4. ______________________________

5. ______________________________

A. **Read the rules of a pioneer school. Check ✔ the ones that are the same as those in your school.**

School Rules

1. Obey and accept consequences by your teacher. ☐
2. Walk quietly into or out of the classroom. ☐
3. Wash your hands at the end of the class. Wash your feet if they are bare. ☐
4. Bring firewood to the classroom when your teacher asks you to. ☐
5. When your teacher calls your name after class, tidy everything in the classroom before leaving. ☐
6. Do not call your classmates names. ☐
7. Do not make noises or disturb your classmates. ☐
8. Do not leave your seat without permission. ☐

Write a rule that you think the pioneer school should have had.

____

Week 4

SOCIAL STUDIES

B. Complete the following statements about lives in pioneer days. Circle the correct word for each statement.

1. Most of the houses were made from ______ .

   A. bricks B. logs C. mud

2. The early settlers learned from the Aboriginal peoples the way to preserve ______ .

   A. meat B. flowers C. fruits

3. They often traded things they needed with ______ .

   A. money B. honey C. sugar

4. As the priests in those days often had to travel from village to village, they were called ______ preachers.

   A. part-time B. roving C. circuit

5. The person who ran a grist mill was called a ______ .

   A. miller B. grister C. grinder

6. A blacksmith made things out of ______ .

   A. coal B. clay C. iron

Who would a pioneer go to when he or she had a toothache but there was no doctor in the village? Circle the correct answer.

A. a teacher B. a blacksmith
C. a priest D. a barber
E. a hunter F. a neighbour

Marshmallow Bunnies

Directions:

1. Glue large marshmallows together as shown.
2. Put toothpick through 1 small marshmallow on each side for arm.
3. Put toothpick through 2 small marshmallows for each ear.
4. Cut out inside ears from construction paper and glue onto marshmallow ears.
5. Put toothpick through 1 small marshmallow for bunny tail.
6. Glue chocolate chips onto face for eyes.

Materials for 1 bunny:

- 2 large marshmallows
- 7 small marshmallows
- toothpicks
- construction paper
- 2 chocolate chips
- thin red licorice
- glue

7. Glue small marshmallow for nose.
8. Cut licorice to 2 cm (x 6) and glue onto marshmallow nose.

A. Read what the children say and draw the shapes on the dot grids.

Leon

I want to draw a quadrilateral with 4 equal sides but it is not a square.

I like parallelograms. I want to draw a parallelogram with 4 right angles.

Linda

David

I want to draw a polygon with 3 sides. It has 1 right angle.

I want to draw a quadrilateral. It looks like a ladder.

Mary

Sue

I want to draw a 3-side polygon. 2 of the sides are with the same length.

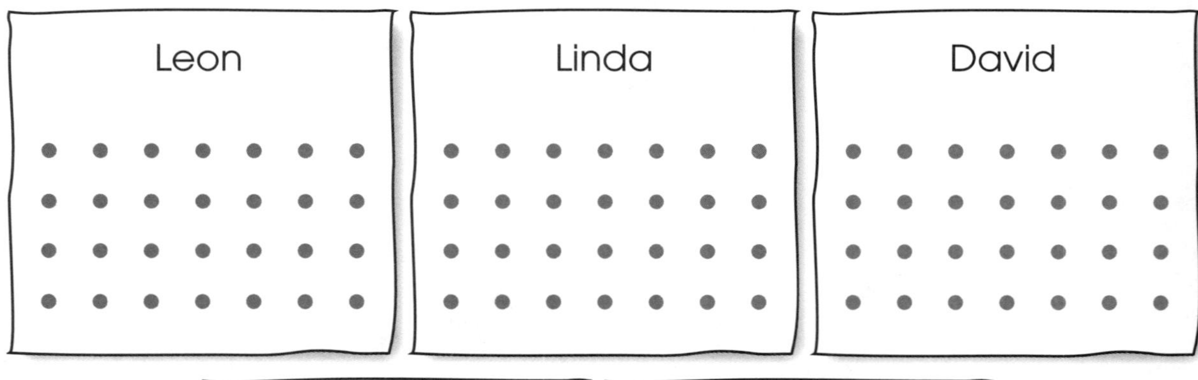

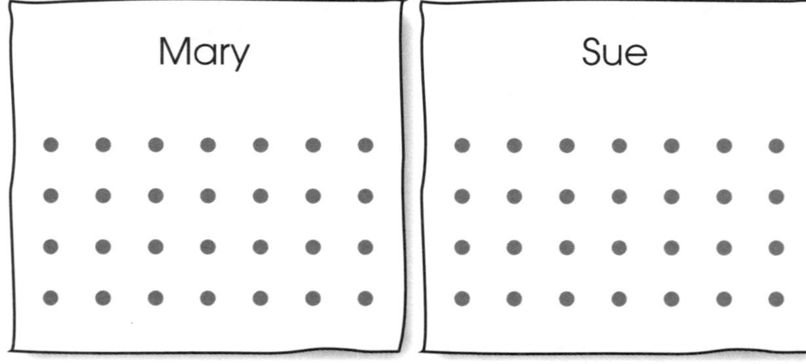

B. Look at the shapes the children made. Help them name the shapes and find the number of faces on each shape.

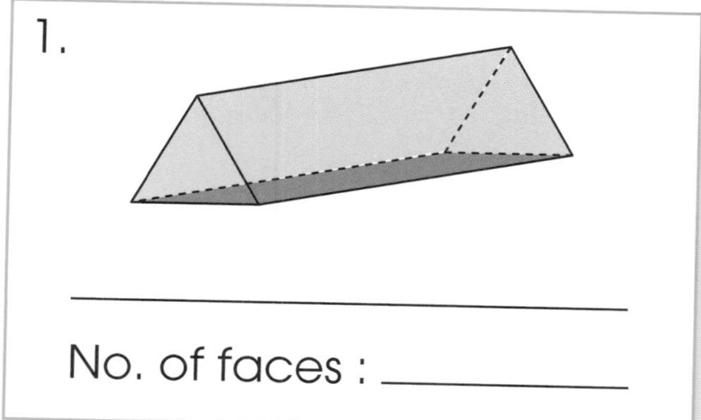

1. ______________________

No. of faces : __________

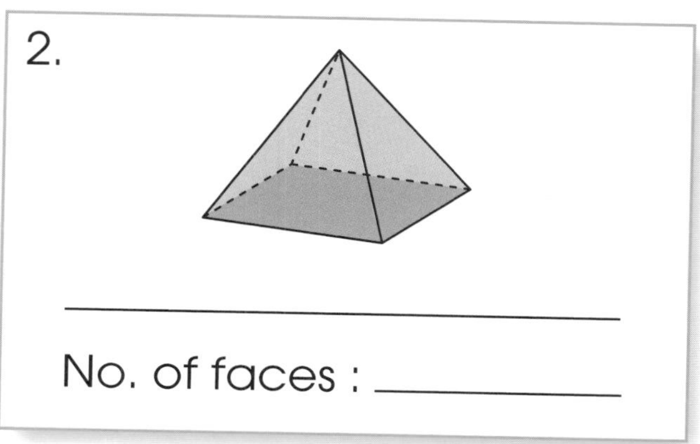

2. ______________________

No. of faces : __________

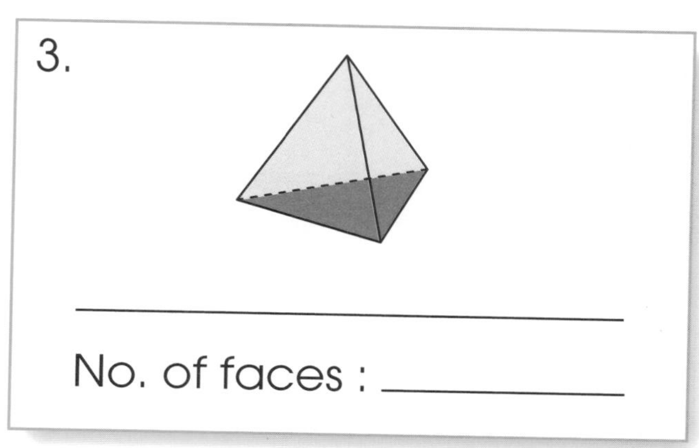

3. ______________________

No. of faces : __________

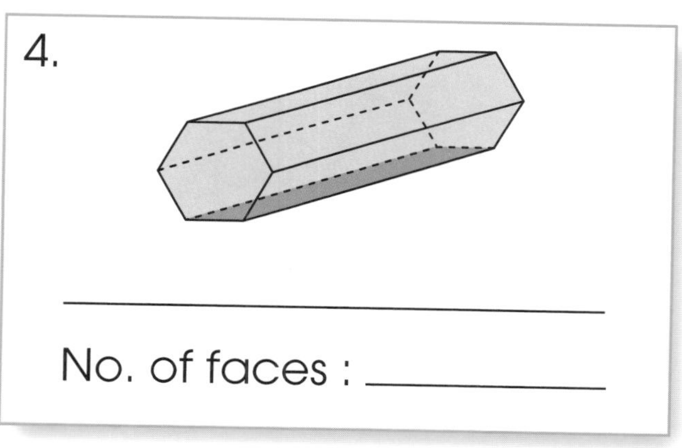

4. ______________________

No. of faces : __________

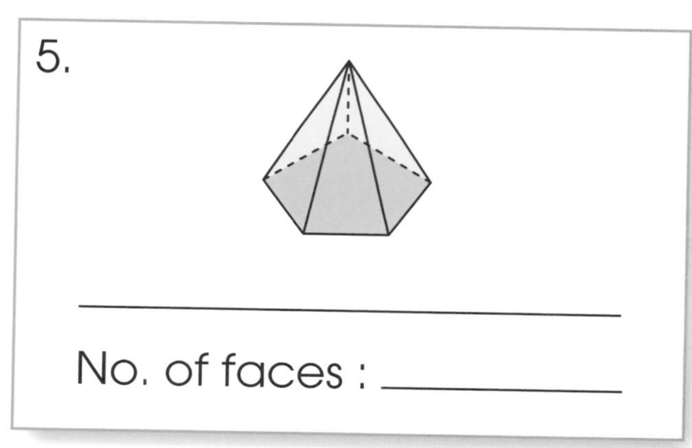

5. ______________________

No. of faces : __________

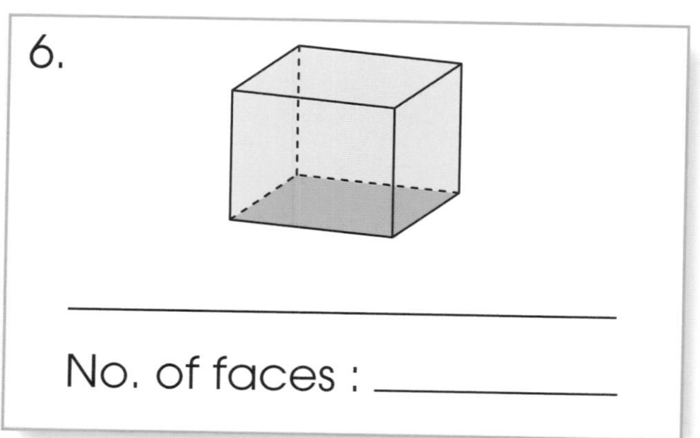

6. ______________________

No. of faces : __________

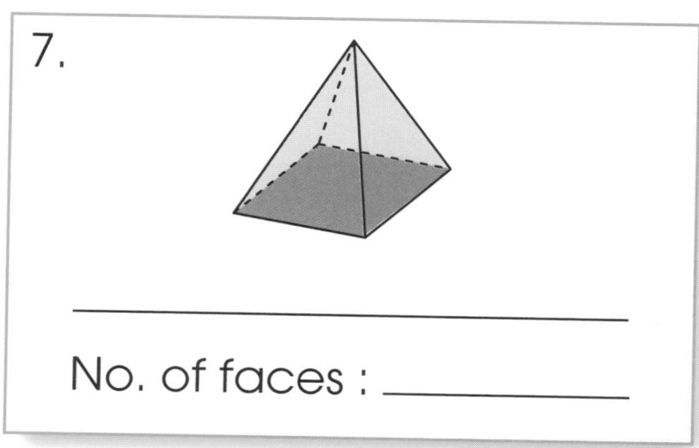

7. ______________________

No. of faces : __________

Week 5

MATHEMATICS

C. The children glue sticks to form patterns. Help each of them continue the pattern and find how many more sticks are needed.

1\.

Leon needs ______ more sticks to extend this pattern to 9 congruent trapezoids.

2\.

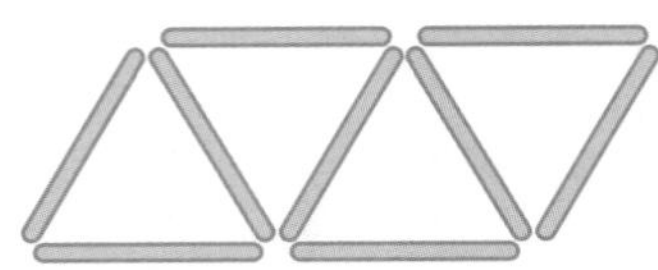

Linda needs ______ more sticks to extend this pattern to 8 congruent triangles.

3\.

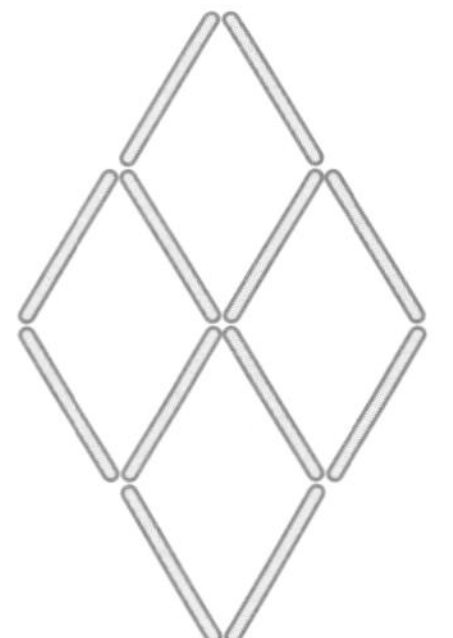

Mary needs ______ more sticks to extend this pattern to 9 congruent rhombuses.

4\.

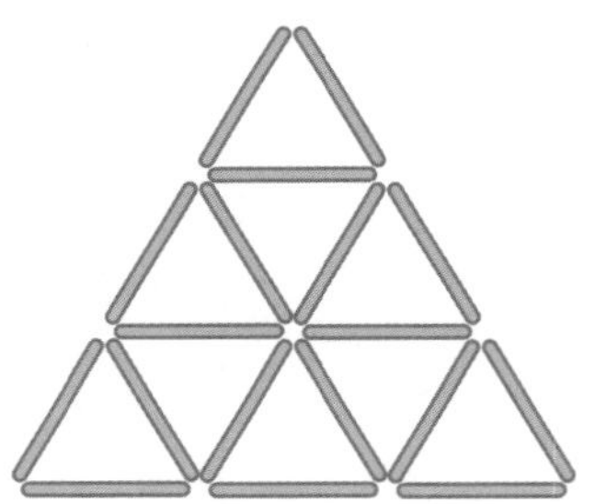

Sue needs ______ more sticks to extend this pattern to 16 congruent triangles.

D. Look at the table to find out how many shapes the children cut. Help them round the numbers to the nearest 10. Then write the rounded numbers in words to complete what the children say.

1.

Children	Mary	David	Linda	Sue	Leon
No. of Shapes	82	91	45	32	57
Rounded to the Nearest 10					

2. Mary : I cut about ______________________ shapes.
3. David : I cut about ______________________ shapes.
4. Linda : I cut about ______________________ shapes.
5. Sue : I cut about ______________________ shapes.
6. Leon : I cut about ______________________ shapes.

Which row of tiles would be the next row in the pattern? Check ✔ the correct letter.

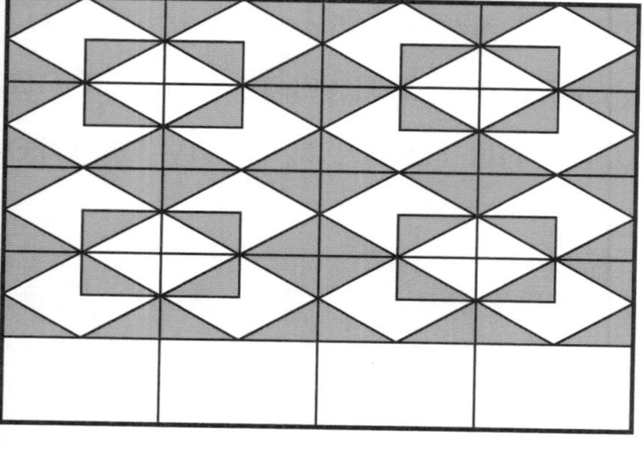

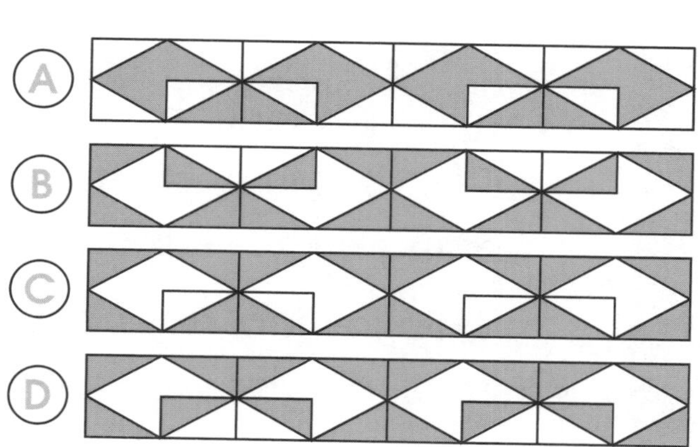

Rollerblading

Rollerblading, also called in-line skating, has become a popular sport. It is a fun activity and a great form of exercise. Rollerblading involves speed, balance, and coordination. Of course, when participating in any sport, there is always the risk of injury. In order to have an enjoyable and safe time rollerblading, it is important to follow some simple guidelines.

Before going out on the rollerblade trail, it is critical to wear the proper equipment. First of all, the rollerblades should be of good quality. They should fit snugly and be laced or buckled tight. This gives support to the ankles. Next, a proper fitting helmet should be worn to protect the head. Wrist guards are important to wear on your hands. They help to absorb the shock of a fall. Elbow and knee pads should also be worn to cushion these body parts in case of a fall.

If you are a beginner, it is a good idea to take a lesson. Practising should be done on a large, flat surface with little or no traffic. It is important to learn to stop and turn properly before heading out on a more challenging trail.

Following rules and guidelines can help make sure that rollerblading is a fun and safe sport for all participants.

A. Check ✔ the true sentences.

1. In-line skating is more popular than rollerblading. ______
2. You should wear protective gear to rollerblade. ______
3. Snugly-fitted rollerblades give support to your ankles. ______
4. In rollerblading, stopping and turning are important skills to learn. ______
5. You should practise rollerblading on a challenging trail. ______
6. Rollerblading is the safest sport for children. ______

B. Answer the following questions.

1. Name another summer activity which must be done outdoors.

   ____

2. Name another sport which requires a helmet to be worn.

   ____

3. Name another sport which uses equipment with wheels.

   ____

4. Name another activity which requires good balance.

   ____

5. Name another sport where taking lessons is recommended.

   ____

C. **Complete the following charts to show the similarities and differences between rollerblading and ice-skating. One example is done.**

Rollerblading and ice-skating are alike in the following ways.

1. They both require balance.
2. ______
3. ______
4. ______
5. ______

Rollerblading and ice-skating are different in the following ways.

Rollerblading:
1. It is done on a pavement.
2. ______
3. ______

Ice-skating:
1. ______
2. ______
3. ______

D. Circle the following words in the word search.

automobile bicycle motorcycle rollerblades
rollerskates scooter skateboard tricycle
unicycle van wagon wheelbarrow

g	r	y	m	l	z	n	v	w	a	n	u	p	h	y	c
u	o	a	t	b	l	a	g	v	s	k	a	w	w	i	r
b	l	r	d	x	e	s	y	p	t	j	t	t	h	o	e
x	l	e	s	r	b	k	s	v	t	y	s	r	e	q	a
o	e	z	b	o	m	a	r	a	r	n	u	i	e	x	v
q	r	m	w	l	q	t	u	n	i	c	y	c	l	e	s
h	s	i	m	l	z	e	m	v	g	w	l	y	b	d	y
y	k	p	o	g	a	b	x	b	t	p	k	c	a	m	h
e	a	u	t	o	m	o	b	i	l	e	t	l	r	q	c
p	t	h	o	q	d	a	s	c	o	o	t	e	r	n	g
o	e	w	r	z	o	r	y	y	i	l	w	i	o	s	f
c	s	j	c	a	m	d	r	c	u	j	o	v	w	t	l
x	d	s	y	v	f	x	q	l	s	w	a	g	o	n	e
a	v	o	c	t	m	g	w	e	z	x	o	y	d	x	s
m	r	o	l	l	e	r	b	l	a	d	e	s	j	v	a
l	s	b	e	t	p	n	o	g	r	l	m	g	w	b	r
u	i	r	z	k	b	c	w	i	u	a	z	f	t	l	v

Stability *is important in our lives. Things that we make should stay the way they are meant to be when forces act upon them.*

Week 5

A. Look at the pictures. Write "stable" for the stable structures and "unstable" for the unstable structures.

B. Write below each picture the effect of the force at work.

Stretch Slide Bend Twist Squeeze

1. ______________

2. ______________

3.

4.

5.

C. Do you want to feel forces in action? Try this!

- Stand with your back and heels up against a wall.
- Have someone place a coin (or some other small object) in front of you on the floor.
- Now, without bending your knees, bend down and pick it up.
- What happened?

You had difficulty because when you bent over to pick up the object, your centre of gravity shifted, and you lost your stability. Normally, when you bend to pick up something, your behind moves backwards, and in this way, maintains the centre of gravity. You remain stable.

Some of the things that people did in Canada in the 1700s were the same as today. Some things were different.

Week 5

SOCIAL STUDIES

A. Check ✔ "Same" if people today do the same. Check ✔ "Different" if they do not.

	Same	Different
1. Boys chop wood.	☐	☐
2. Women cook meals.	☐	☐
3. Men hunt for food.	☐	☐
4. Families ride in buggies.	☐	☐
5. Children play with hoops.	☐	☐
6. People make their own candles.	☐	☐
7. Children use slates and chalk.	☐	☐
8. Boys and girls play tag.	☐	☐
9. People grow their own vegetables.	☐	☐
10. Fathers and mothers have jobs.	☐	☐

Pioneer children had toys and games. We still play some of them today.

B. Write the name of the toy or game under each picture. Colour the ones that we still play today.

Hoops | Sack Races | Hopscotch
Marbles | Tic Tac Toe | Spinning Tops

1

____

2

____

3

____

4

____

5

____

6

____

Did you know that in pioneer days, marbles were made of clay, and were used in numerous games?

Ladybug Paperweight

Materials:

- glue
- paintbrushes
- small piece of felt
- smooth beach stone
- spray or flat sealant
- black, red, yellow paint

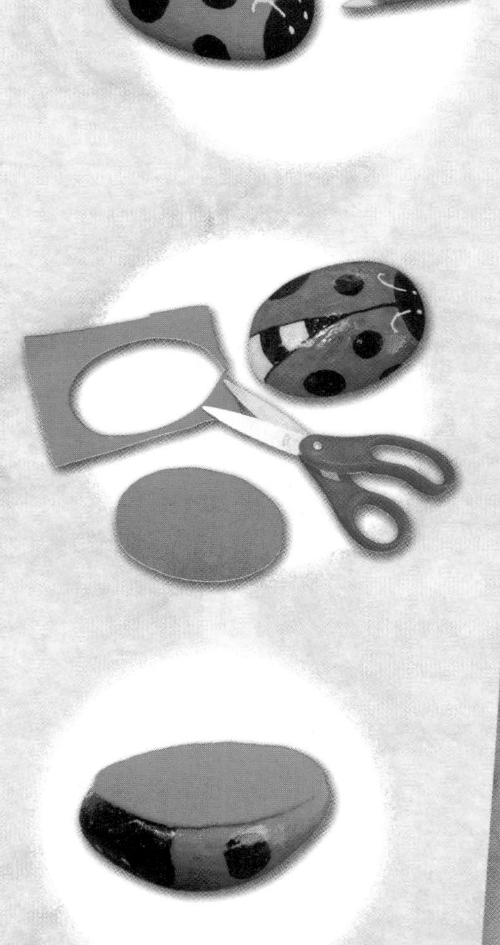

Directions:

1. Spread out newspaper.
2. Paint beach stone red. Let dry.
3. Using fine brush, paint ladybug as shown. Let dry.
4. Spray or paint with clear sealant.
5. Spray underside.
6. Cut small piece of felt.
7. Glue felt to underside of ladybug.

A. Look at the different packets of orange juice. Help Jacky name the shapes of the containers. Then answer the questions.

1.	
Ⓐ Orange Juice 2 L; Ⓑ 150 mL; Ⓒ Juice 450 mL; Ⓓ Juice 100 mL; Ⓔ 1 L Orange Juice; Ⓕ Juice 200 mL; Ⓖ 300 mL Orange Juice	Ⓐ ________ Ⓑ ________ Ⓒ ________ Ⓓ ________ Ⓔ ________ Ⓕ ________ Ⓖ ________

1 L of juice can fill 4 glasses.

2. Which container has the greatest capacity? ______

3. Which container has the least capacity? ______

4. How many containers have a capacity less than 1 L? ______

5. How many packets of Ⓔ are needed to fill 12 glasses of juice? ______

6. A big bottle can hold 20 glasses of juice. How many packets of Ⓐ are needed to fill a bottle? ______

B. Write the cost of each packet of juice in decimal notation. Then answer the children's questions.

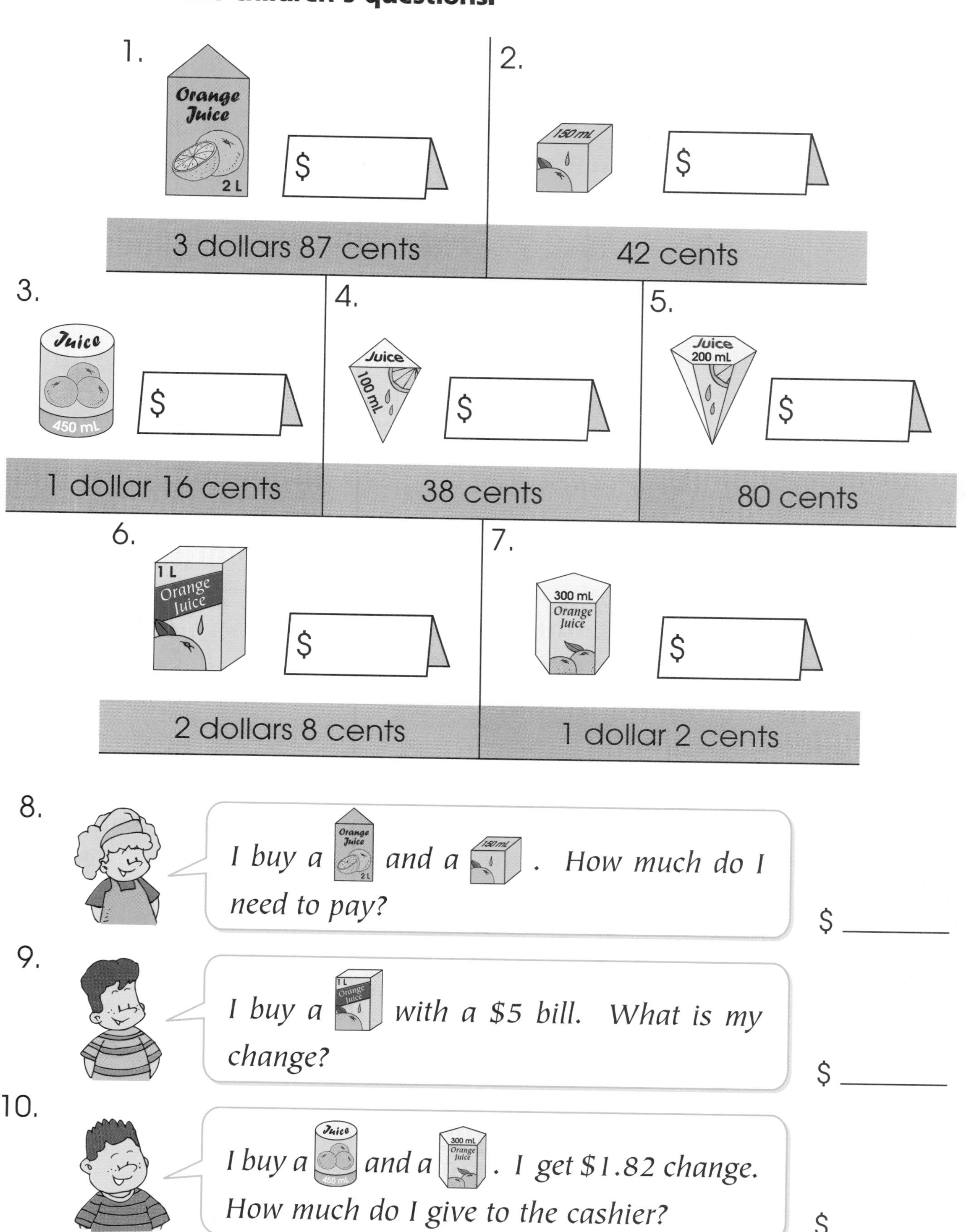

C. Read what Susan and her friends say. Help them complete the tables and solve the problems.

1. *I buy 50 packets of orange juice for my family. We drink 4 packets every day.*

a.

Day	1	2	3	4
No. of Packets Left	46			

b. ______ packets will be left after 6 days.

2. *I box can hold 8 packets. I want to buy 8 boxes.*

a.

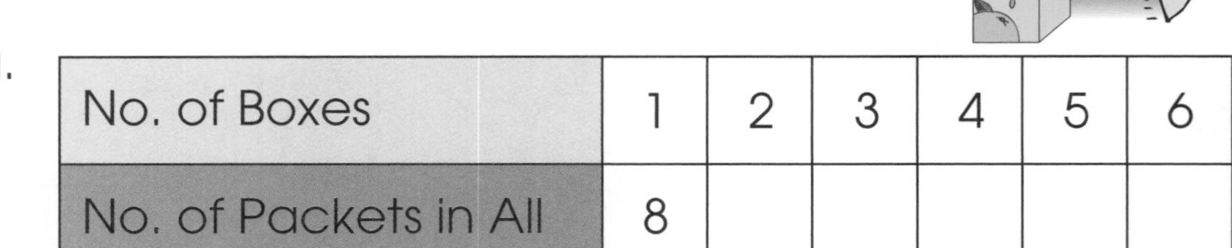

No. of Boxes	1	2	3	4	5	6
No. of Packets in All	8					

b. There are ______ packets in 8 boxes.

3. *I can fill a jug with 5 packets.*

a.

No. of Jugs	1	2	3	4
No. of Packets Needed	5			

b. ______ packets are needed to fill 6 jugs.

D. See how many packets of orange juice Jacky has. Then colour the pictures to show the packets each child gets from Jacky and write the numbers.

1. Jacky gives $\frac{1}{2}$ of his (juice) to Sue.

a.

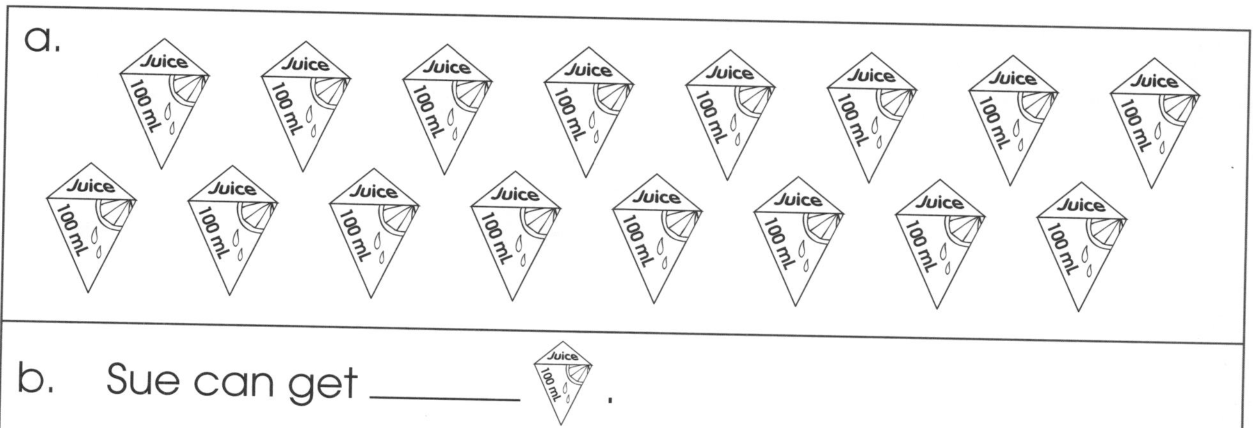

b. Sue can get ______ (juice) .

2. Jacky gives $\frac{1}{3}$ of his (juice box) to Mabel.

a.

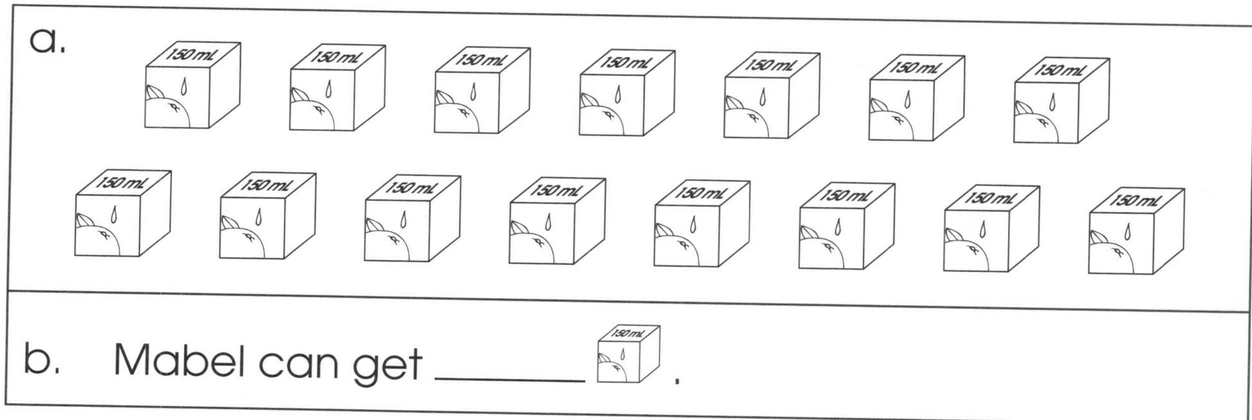

b. Mabel can get ______ (juice box) .

BRAIN TEASER

Write a fraction to tell how much each figure is coloured.

1.

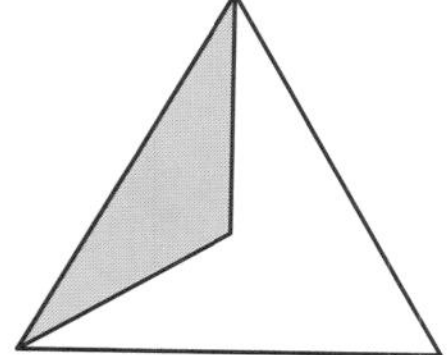

______

2.

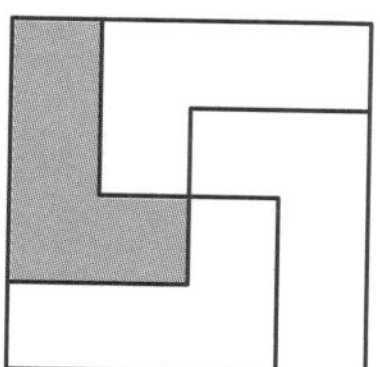

______

3.

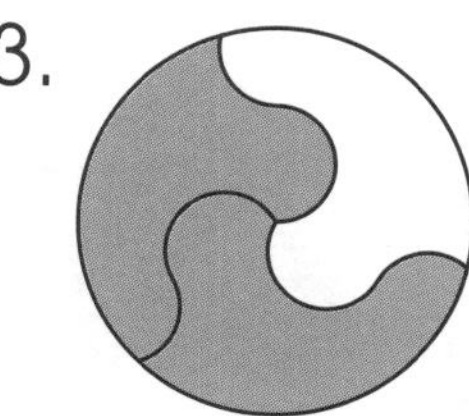

______

What I Didn't Do During *Summer Vacation*

It was summer vacation, the time for new adventures, the time to see new places, and the time to make memories that would last a lifetime. There were so many things I wanted to do.

I wanted to go white water rafting on the Ottawa River. My mother said it was too dangerous so I didn't go. I wanted to swim across Lake Ontario. My swimming coach told me that first I would have to be able to swim across the pool. I couldn't, so I didn't swim across Lake Ontario. I wanted to fly to Nepal and climb Mount Everest, the tallest mountain in the world. My teacher told me that it would take too long and I would miss too many days of school. So, I didn't climb Mount Everest.

During summer vacation, I didn't do a lot of the things I wanted to do. I did, however, go camping and I did stay in a cottage on Pigeon Lake for a week. I did spend an entire day at Canada's Wonderland. I spent many hours with my friends rollerblading, biking, hiking, and splashing in the pool. During my summer vacation, I had new adventures, I saw new places, and I created memories that would last a lifetime.

A. Answer the following questions.

1. Why didn't the writer go white water rafting?

2. Why couldn't the writer swim across Lake Ontario?

3. What is so special about Mount Everest?

4. Name one thing that the writer actually did during summer vacation.

5. Do you think the writer enjoyed her summer vacation? Why?

B. Find the synonyms of the following words from the passage.

1. holiday: ____________
2. skip: ____________
3. cycling: ____________
4. made: ____________
5. instructor: ____________
6. whole: ____________
7. highest: ____________
8. unsafe: ____________

C. **Think about your summer vacation and complete the following lists.**

Things I Wanted to Do	Things I Actually Did

D. **Using the information from the lists, write your own story about your summer vacation.**

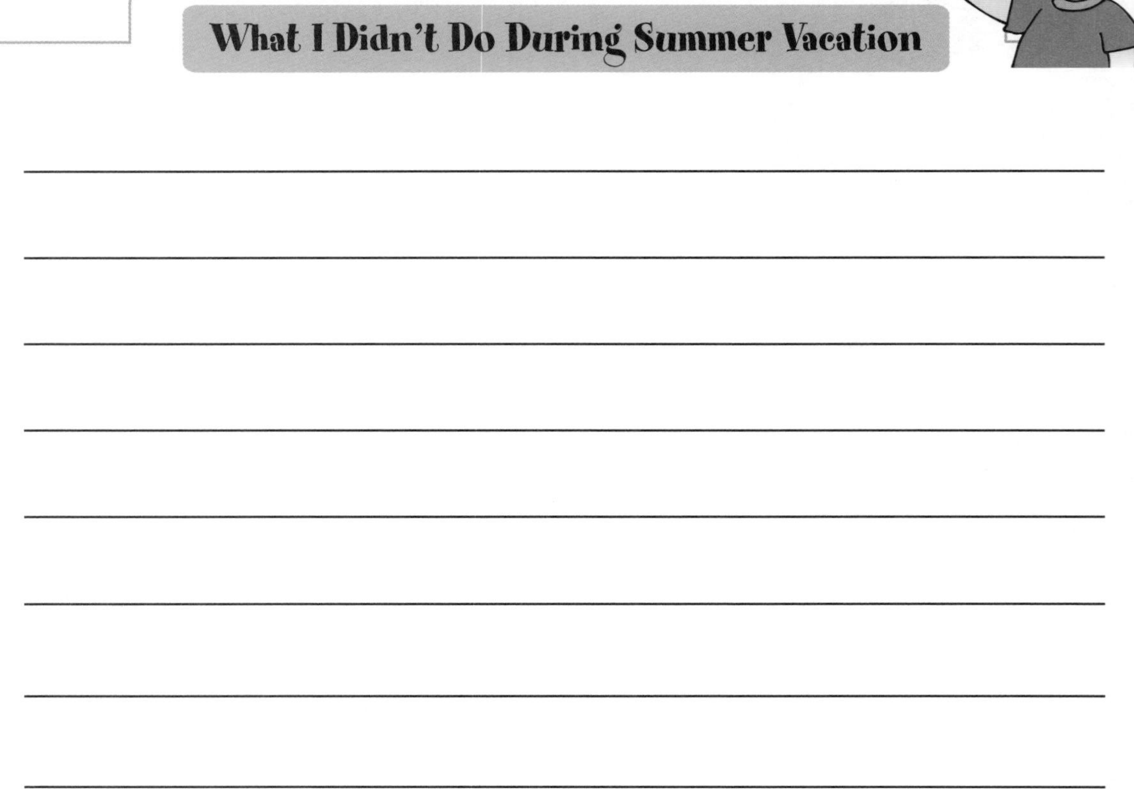

E. Rewrite each sentence changing the underlined words to a contraction.

1. I can not play street hockey this afternoon.

   ____

2. Maria could not find her sunglasses.

   ____

3. I have read stories about Mount Everest.

   ____

4. It is wonderful to sleep in during the week.

   ____

5. We are going to go camping in Algonquin Park.

   ____

F. Complete each statement in the box and then draw a scene to match what is being said. Try to make your statements funny.

During my summer vacation I really wanted to climb Mount Everest. Instead I climbed a tree in my backyard.

During summer vacation I really wanted to...

Instead I...

Soil: More Than Dirt

A. Here's the recipe for soil, but only four ingredients are correct. Check ✔ the right ingredients.

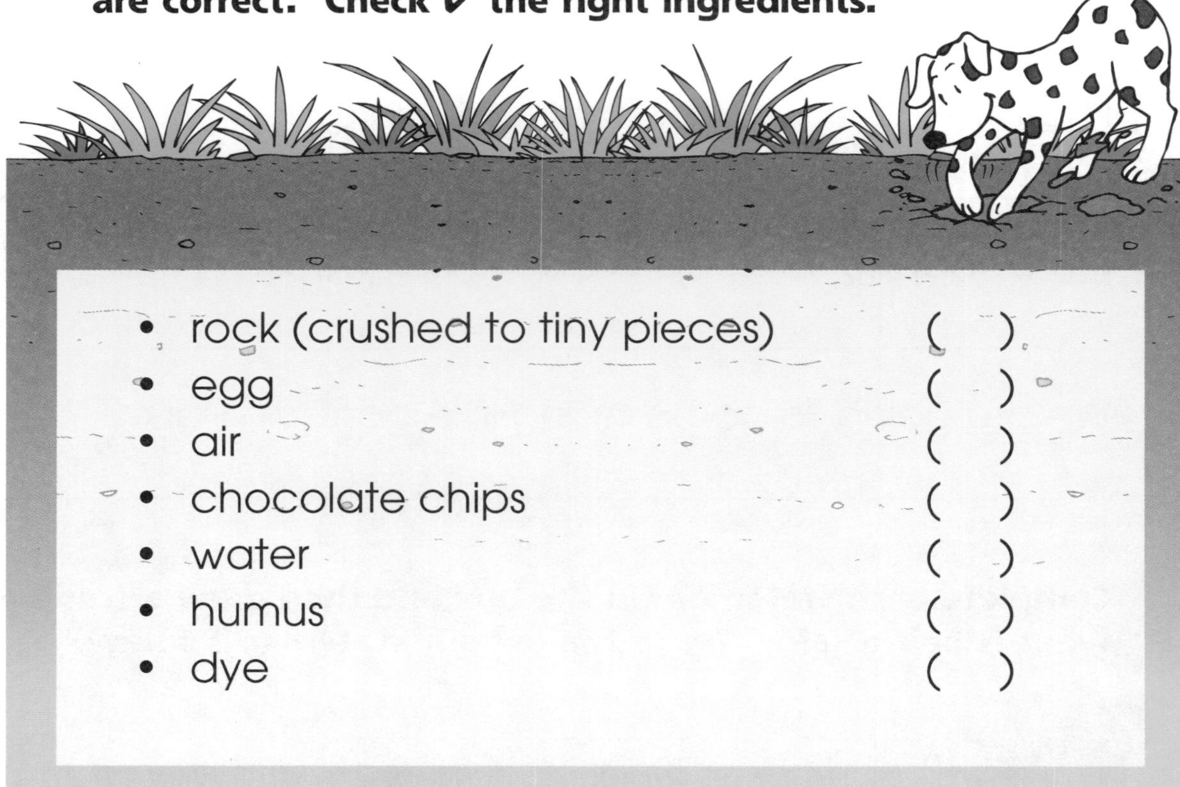

- rock (crushed to tiny pieces) ( )
- egg ( )
- air ( )
- chocolate chips ( )
- water ( )
- humus ( )
- dye ( )

B. Try this!

Can you see the air in soil? Here's how you can. Fill a clear jar about half way with soil. Add water. Do you see bubbles? That is the air rising as the water takes up the spaces that the air took.

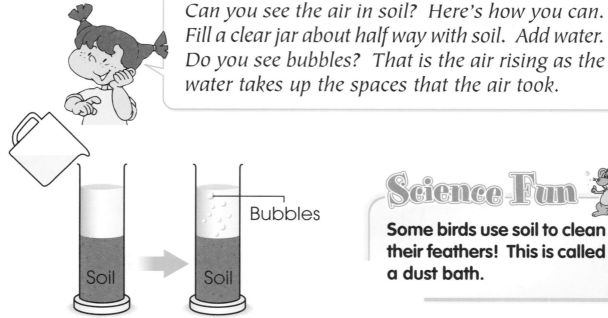

Science Fun

Some birds use soil to clean their feathers! This is called a dust bath.

Humus *in soil is good for growing plants because of the nutrients it contains. In nature, humus is made from decaying plants or animal remains. We make humus when we compost.*

C. The following things, with their peels and clippings, are what we might throw into a compost bin. Find them and circle them in the word search.

vegetables grass plants
tea bags fruit
leaves soil egg shells
coffee grounds

Science Fun

The rock in soil has been broken down over millions of years to the size of sand, or smaller. Silt is smaller than sand, and clay is smaller still.

a	w	o	l	j	e	m	i	g	c	r	b	o
c	o	f	f	e	e	g	r	o	u	n	d	s
w	p	v	e	g	e	t	a	b	l	e	s	p
e	l	d	w	g	r	a	s	s	r	h	o	q
j	a	f	h	s	k	g	a	s	y	l	i	m
t	n	s	b	h	c	f	r	u	i	t	l	w
x	t	j	t	e	a	b	a	g	s	p	y	b
u	s	a	e	l	e	a	v	e	s	x	c	l
o	h	g	i	l	f	w	r	q	k	m	a	c
b	y	t	r	s	a	d	i	b	e	g	f	k

A. **This is an urban community. Draw the buildings and vehicles on the map in the locations given.**

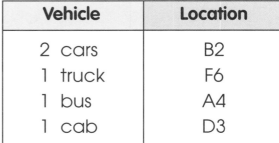

Vehicle	Location
2 cars	B2
1 truck	F6
1 bus	A4
1 cab	D3

Building	Location
1 hospital	C5
1 school	E4
2 houses	H6
1 highrise building	G1

	1	2	3	4	5	6
A						
B						
C						
D						
E						
F						
G						
H						

Communities *can be rural as well. People in rural areas live by farming, fishing, cutting down trees, or mining.*

B. Complete the crossword puzzle with words related to rural communities.

Across

A. This vehicle is for transporting goods.
B. Fruit trees are grown there.
C. a heap of dried grass
D. where minerals are dug out

Down

1. where crops or animal food are kept
2. It's for pulling farm machinery.
3. a tall, round tower for storing grain
4. a kind of fishing boat

Ziploc® Aquarium

Materials:

- Ziploc® bag
- blue food colouring
- gummy fish or confetti fish (at party stores)
- water
- permanent markers

Directions:

1. Draw picture of marine plants on bag with permanent markers.
2. Fill bag $\frac{3}{4}$ full with water.
3. Put 1 drop of blue food colouring into water and mix.
4. Add fish.
5. Squish gently and watch fish "swim".

A. **Anna goes shopping with Daisy. Help the girls write the prices in decimals. Then complete the table.**

Paintbrush	4 dollars 60 cents	**Tube paint**	2 dollars 44 cents
Ruler	1 dollar 9 cents	**Scissors**	95 cents
Stapler	3 dollars 49 cents	**Pencil case**	2 dollars 89 cents

1.

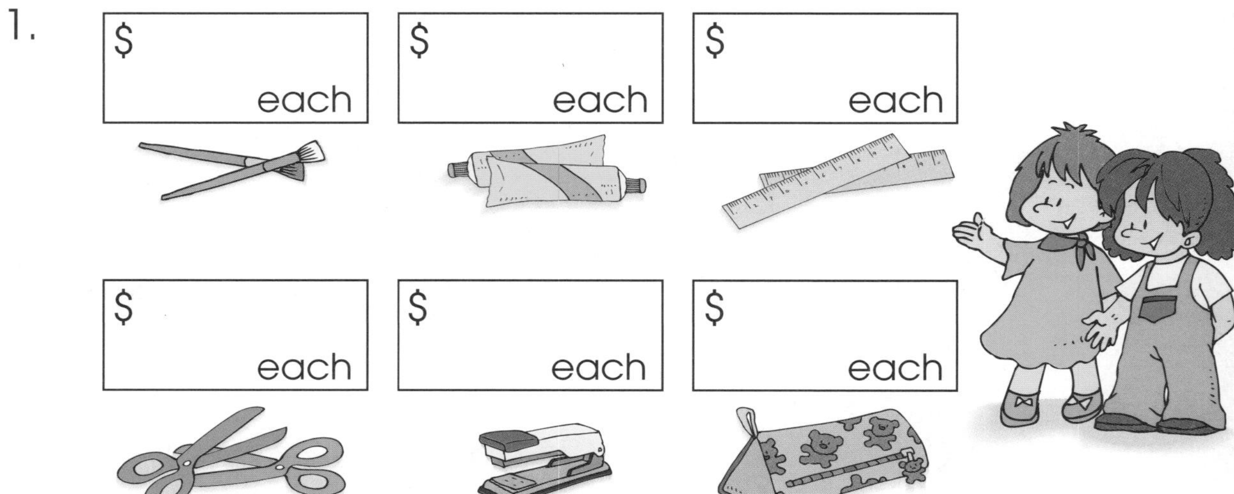

		Cost	Pay with	Change
2.	(paintbrush and scissors)		(5-dollar bill and 1-dollar coin)	
3.	(stapler and ruler)		(three 2-dollar coins)	
4.	(pencil case and tube paints)		(10-dollar bill)	

B. Lucy gets some raffle tickets from buying the things. Help her colour the tickets and do the skill questions. Then answer her question.

1. **A** **Colour the numbers that are divisible by 5.**

213	30	99	90	63	22	25	55	40
552	10	43	35	108	49	68	84	85
92	20	15	5	70	457	75	45	60
56	32	72	80	503	9	100	752	37
27	356	102	65	6	207	95	50	105

465 + 296 = ________

510 + 114 = ________

327 – 285 = ________

853 – 691 = ________

2. **B** **Colour the numbers that are divisible by 2.**

13	11	16	81	24	30	42	31	3
55	73	4	11	2	13	83	61	43
17	99	8	27	10	6	28	79	87
73	67	20	35	14	37	44	13	9
49	51	12	5	38	26	50	67	15

6 x 5 = ________

2 x 7 = ________

4 x 9 = ________

8 x 3 = ________

3. **C** **Colour the numbers that are divisible by 10.**

72	66	32	10	50	40	2	26	42
5	48	13	25	22	60	52	47	8
23	17	84	30	70	80	63	54	93
45	28	62	20	36	31	7	15	72
87	96	36	150	100	90	14	67	39

700 – 85 = ________

663 – 319 = ________

274 + 196 = ________

511 + 206 = ________

4. *If the hidden number on the puzzle is the same as one of the answers to the skill questions, I can get a prize. Which ticket can win a prize?*

Raffle ticket ________ can win a prize.

C. **Look at the box of chocolates that Lucy won. Help her write whole numbers or fractions to complete the sentences.**

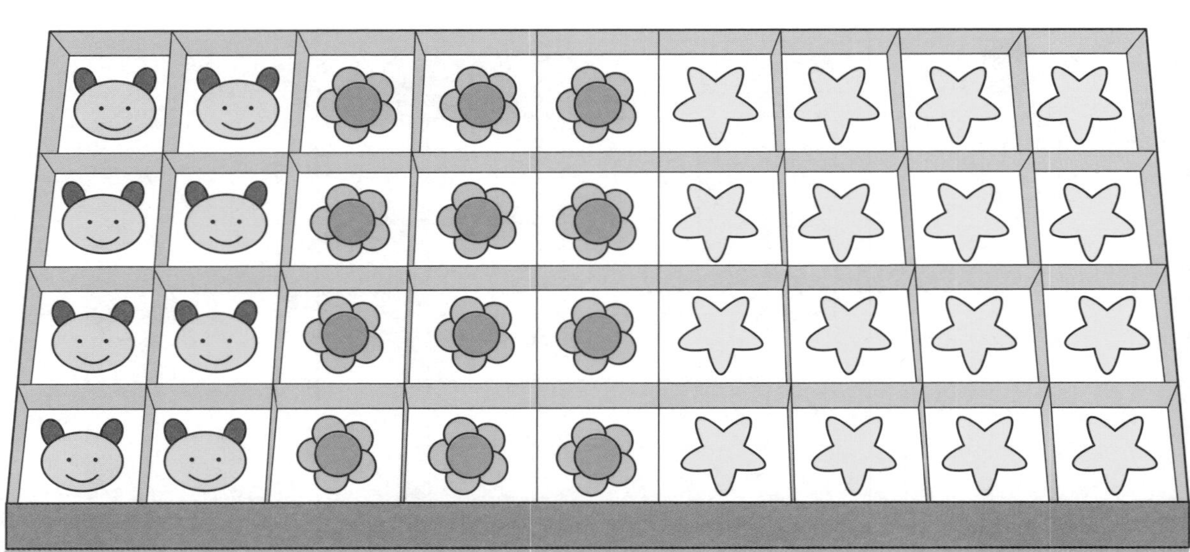

1. There are 4 rows of ________ chocolates; there are ________ chocolates in all.

2. ________ out of ________ chocolates or ________ of a box of chocolates are (bear chocolate).

3. ________ out of ________ chocolates or ________ of a box of chocolates are (flower chocolate).

4. If Lucy divides the (star chocolate) into 2 equal groups, there are ________ (star chocolate) in each group.

5. $\frac{1}{2}$ of the (bear chocolate) or ________ (bear chocolate) are with nuts.

6. $\frac{1}{2}$ of the (star chocolate) or ________ (star chocolate) are with fruit.

7. If Lucy gives $\frac{1}{2}$ of the box of chocolates to Daisy, Daisy will get ________ chocolates.

D. Lucy is writing numbers on her chocolate box. Follow her pattern to complete each row and describe the changes.

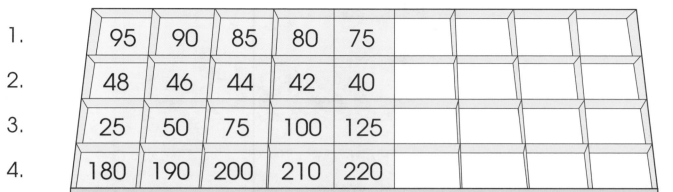

1.	95	90	85	80	75				
2.	48	46	44	42	40				
3.	25	50	75	100	125				
4.	180	190	200	210	220				

5. Row 1: Each number increases / decreases by ______ .

6. Row 2: Each number increases / decreases by ______ .

7. Row 3: Each number increases / decreases by ______ .

8. Row 4: Each number increases / decreases by ______ .

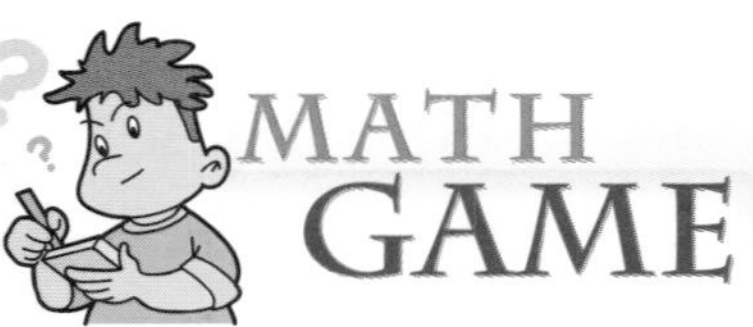

Draw John's route. Then find where he is going.

Home → North, 2 km → East, 4 km → South, 4 km → West, 2 km → North, 1 km → West, 4 km

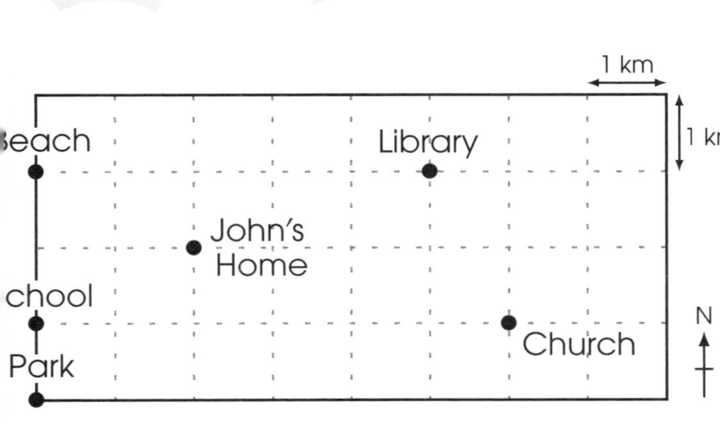

I am going to ______________ .

Larry's Adventure in the Castle

Larry sat at the back of the yellow school bus. It was a very bumpy ride but it was all worth it. Today, Larry's class was visiting a real castle.

The bus finally came to a stop in front of a magnificent building. Larry could not believe his eyes. The castle was identical to the ones that he had been studying in class.

Mr. Pitterson greeted the students on the stairs. He was going to lead the tour through the castle. He explained to the students that they would be seeing many old and interesting artifacts. He also warned them not to wander off alone because it was very easy to get lost in this old, enormous building.

Larry was not listening. He was far too busy staring at something standing at the end of a long corridor. Larry slowly moved closer to examine the object. It was a large, silver suit of armour. Beside the armour was a closed door with a large sign. On the sign were the words, "DO NOT ENTER". Larry felt his hand moving toward the doorknob...

A. Answer the following questions.

1. How did the writer describe the trip to the castle?

____

____

2. Why did Mr. Pitterson tell the children not to wander off alone?

____

____

3. What caught Larry's attention in the castle?

____

____

4. Write out a sentence in the story that shows that Larry was very curious.

____

____

B. Add quotation marks to the following sentences.

1. The teacher said, The castle is very old and historic.
2. Let's go into this room, shouted Larry.
3. How long will the bus ride be? asked the class.
4. I enjoyed the trip, said Brian.
5. The bus driver declared, We are almost at the castle.

C. **Using the following questions as a guide, write an exciting ending to the story. Draw a picture to go with it. Suggest a new title for the story.**

- *What adventure lay behind the closed door?*
- *What happened to Larry?*
- *How did Larry get back to his classmates?*

New Title: ______________________

Week 7

ENGLISH

D. Read the clues and complete the crossword puzzle with words from the passage.

Across

A. passageway
B. rough and uncomfortable
C. works of art
D. protective covering
E. spectacular, wonderful

Down

1. the same
2. looking intensely at
3. huge, gigantic

***Friction** is the resistance to motion between two surfaces in contact.*

Friction

A. Complete the sentences with the words given.

more rough force friction less

1. When we walk across a slippery floor with socks on, there is little ______________ , and we may slip.

2. When tires on a bike have worn down, there is ______________ friction between the tires and the road. The bike may skid easily.

3. The bottom of hiking boots is ______________ , so there is good friction between the boots and the ground.

4. When you need one thing to grip to another, you need ______________ friction.

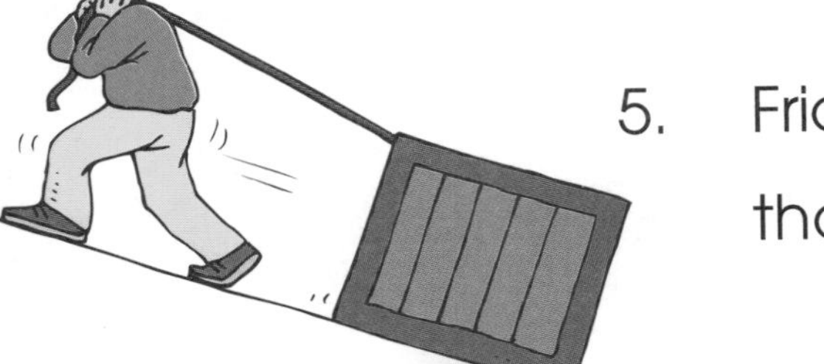

5. Friction is a ______________ that slows down moving things.

Week 7

SCIENCE

B. **Each toy car is exactly the same but each is moving on a different track. Make your prediction. Place the toy cars in the order from 1–5 you think they would be.**

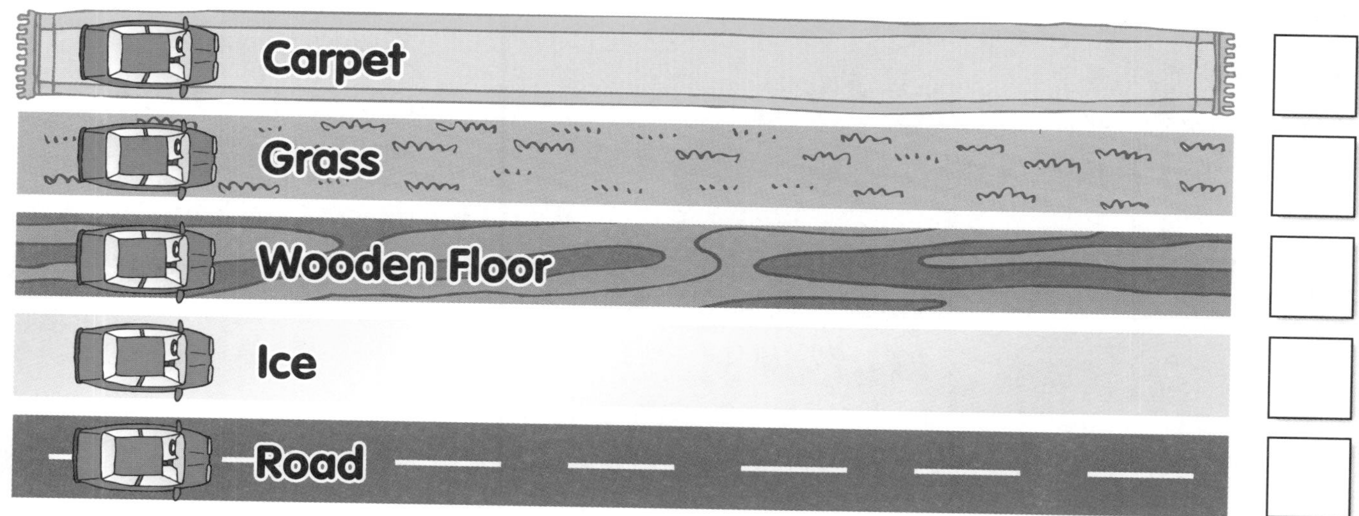

C. **Grip or slip? Each pair of things below may grip to each other if there is enough friction between them. If there is, write "grip" on the line. If not, write "slip".**

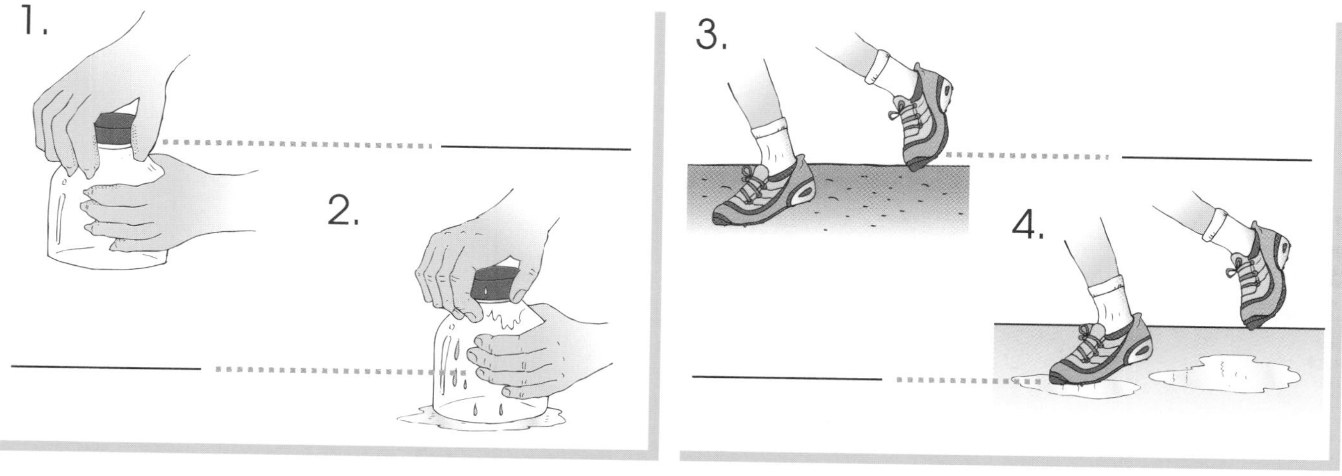

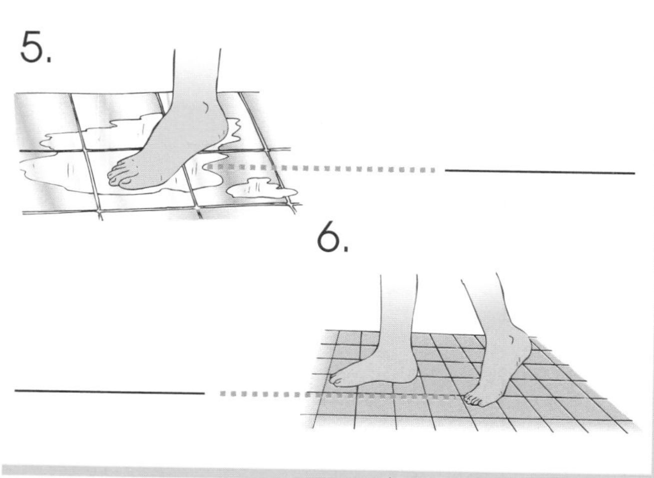

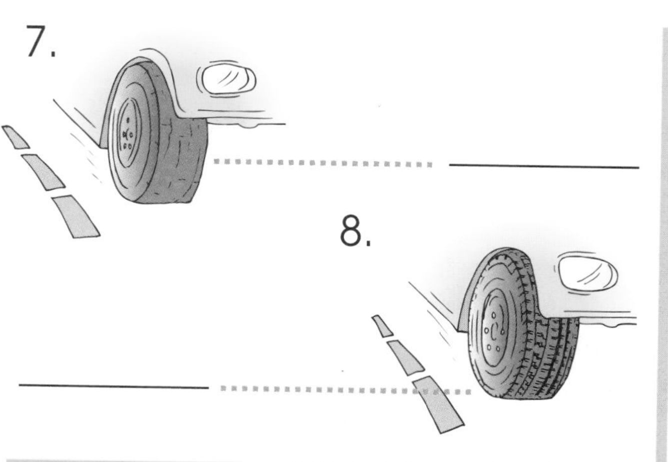

A. **Complete what Aunt Mandy says about Canada with the words from the flag.**

Great Britain
government three
Canada Day
Dominion provinces
ten independent

For a time, Canada belonged to 1.____________ . Then some people in Canada wanted to have their own 2.____________ . After much negotiation, the British government finally approved a plan on July 1, 1867 that allowed Canada to become an 3.____________ country. The new country was named the 4.____________ of Canada. However, it was unlike the Canada we know today. It was made up only of four 5.____________ : Ontario, Quebec, Nova Scotia, and New Brunswick. Now, there are 6.____________ provinces and 7.____________ territories in Canada, and we celebrate 8.____________ on July 1 every year.

B. Write the names of the provinces and territories.

1. ____________________
2. ____________________
3. ____________________
4. ____________________
5. ____________________
6. ____________________
7. ____________________
8. ____________________
9. ____________________
10. ____________________
11. ____________________
12. ____________________
13. ____________________

The word "Canada" comes from the Aboriginal word "kanata" which means "village".

C. Write three facts about the province or territory in which you and your family live.

1. ____________________
____
2. ____________________
____
3. ____________________
____

Penny Pendant

Week 7

ARTS & CRAFTS

Materials

- scissors
- hole punch
- string or yarn
- construction paper of different colours
- glue
- a penny

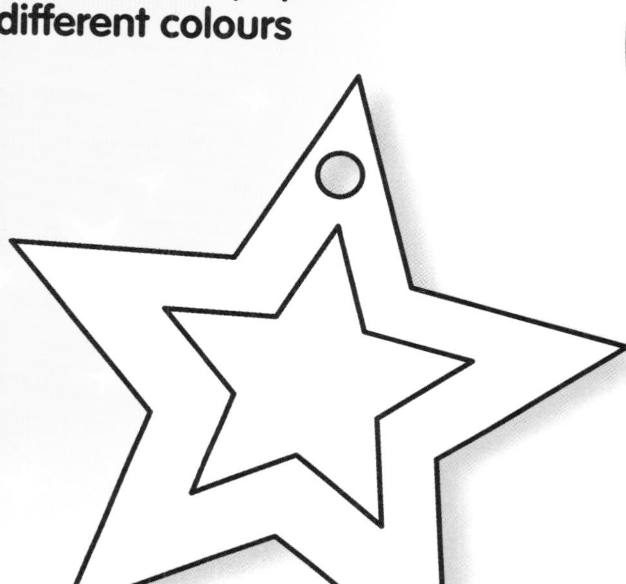

Directions

1. Using tracer, trace small star and cut out.
2. Cut out a bigger star of a different colour.
3. Glue the small star onto the big star.
4. Glue penny in the middle of the stars.
5. Punch a hole near the top of pendant.
6. Thread yarn through pendant.

Week

8

MATHEMATICS

A. **The children are talking about the possibility of some events. Write "possible" or "impossible" on the lines.**

1. 

Mandy can hop 100 times in 1 second.

____

2. 

George can hold his breath for 15 minutes.

____

3. 

Mabel can finish her dinner in 30 minutes.

____

4. 

Tim can trade 4 quarters for a loonie.

____

5. 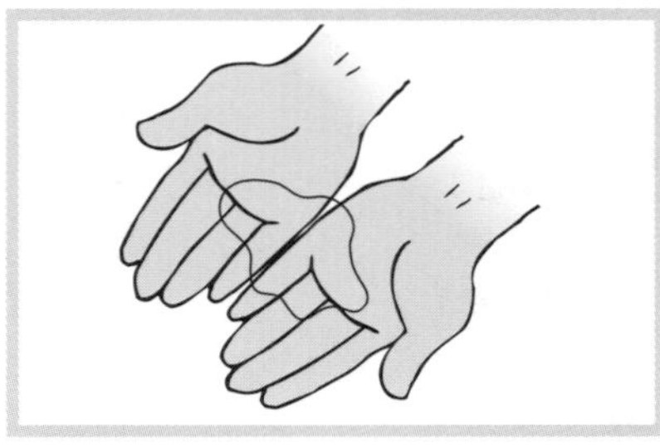

Michael can hold 1 L of water with his hands.

____

6. 

Wilson can pick 1 red marble from a bag of 5 red marbles and 5 green marbles.

____

B. John and his friends are playing with a spinner. Look at the spinner. Help the children check ✔ the correct sentences and cross ✘ the wrong ones.

1. The spinner is most likely to stop on  . ______

2. The spinner is least likely to stop on . ______

3. The best word to describe the chance of the spinner stopping on is "impossible". ______

4. The spinner has a chance to stop on  . ______

5. The spinner has a greater chance to stop on "Please try again!" than . ______

6. The spinner will never stop on . ______

7. John says, "The spinner stopped on last time. I don't think it will stop on again." ______

8. Elaine says, "If the spinner is spun 20 times, I think it may stop on 5 times." ______

C. John and his friends are playing with a box of 12 marbles. Help the children colour the marbles. Then answer the questions.

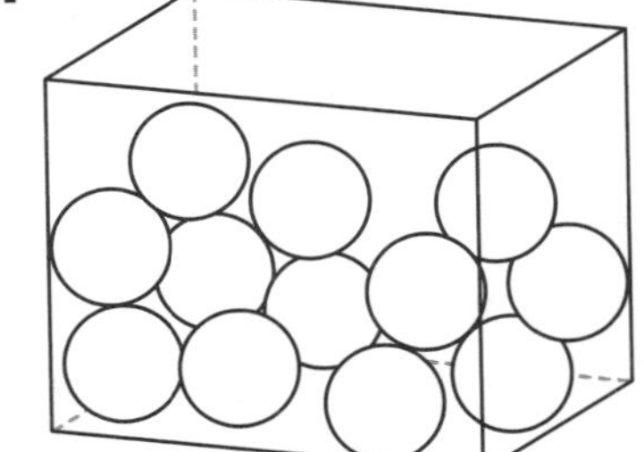

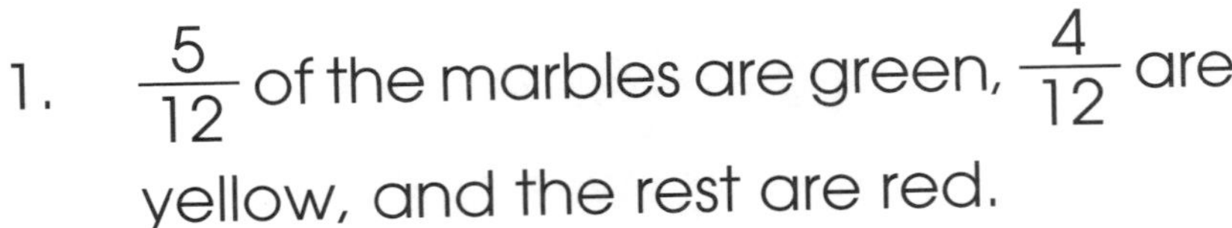

1. $\frac{5}{12}$ of the marbles are green, $\frac{4}{12}$ are yellow, and the rest are red.

2. Is it possible for the children to pick a red marble? ____________

3. Is it possible for the children to pick a purple marble? ____________

4. Is there a greater chance to pick a red or a green marble? ____________

5. Is there a smaller chance to pick a green or a yellow marble? ____________

6. If Mabel draws a marble from the box, what colour is most likely to be drawn? ____________

7. If John divides his marbles equally into 2 groups, how many marbles will there be in each group? ____________

8. If John divides his marbles equally into 2 groups and puts all the yellow marbles into one group, in how many ways can John divide his marbles? Show all the combinations.

1st Group	2nd Group
4 yellow, ____ green	____ green, ____ red

Week 8

MATHEMATICS

D. John weighs his toys with his marbles. See how heavy each type of marble weighs. Help John record the weights of his toys.

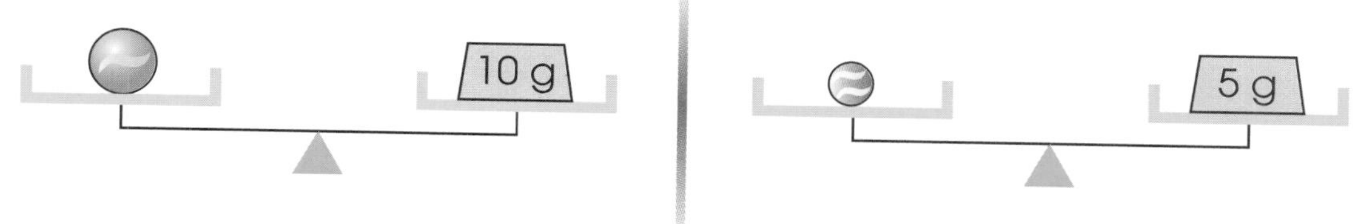

1.

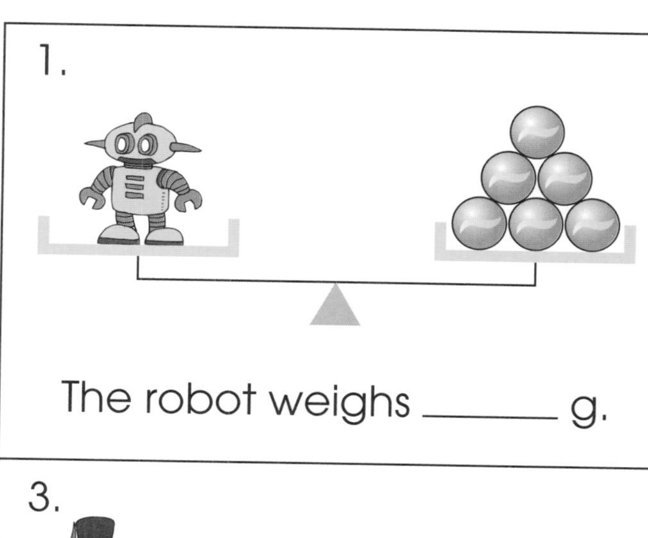

The robot weighs _______ g.

2.

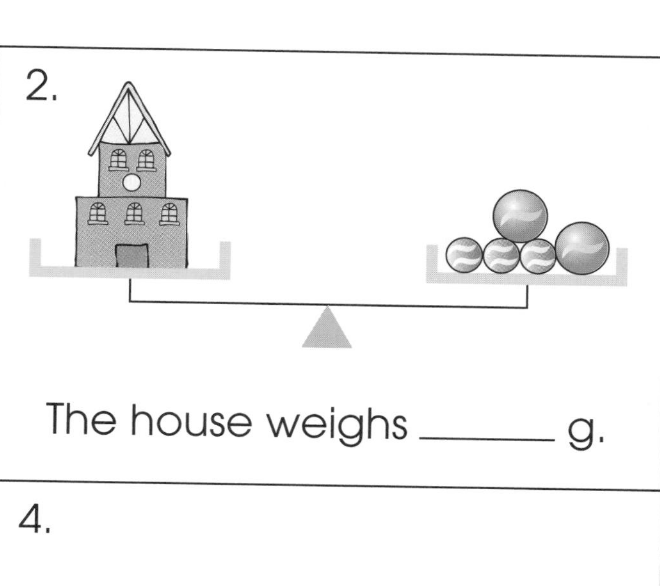

The house weighs _______ g.

3.

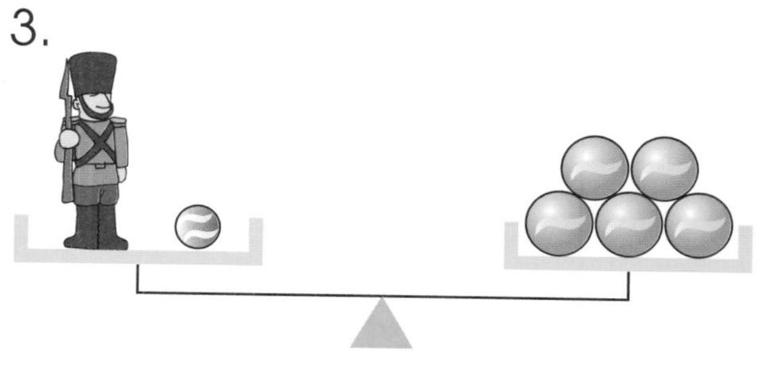

The soldier weighs _______ g.

4.

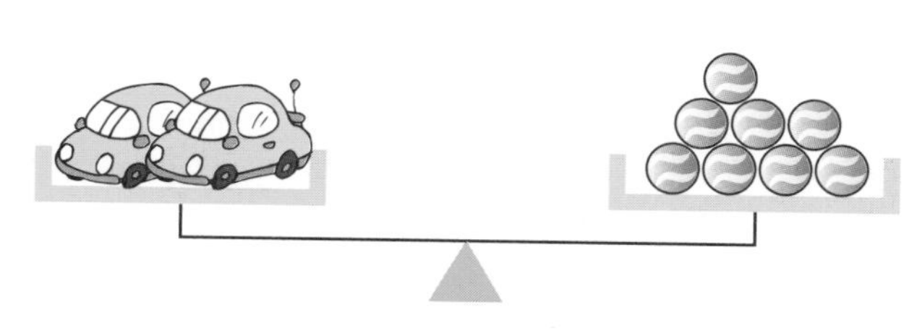

Each car weighs _______ g.

Look at the dartboard. Solve the problem.

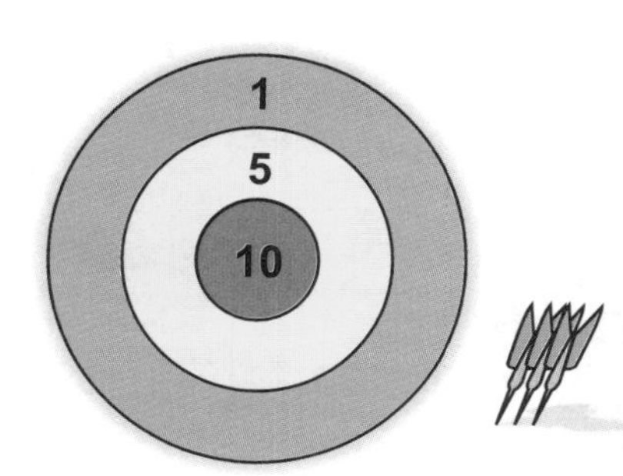

Three darts are thrown. If all the darts hit the dartboard and the points are added up, what are the possible total scores?

The possible total scores are ______________________________.

THE Time Capsule

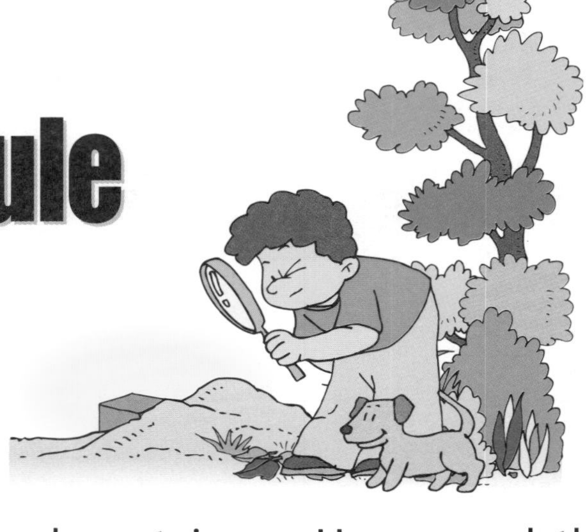

Daniel could hardly believe his luck. He had been planting trees with his father in the backyard when he suddenly uncovered an unusual container. He opened the container and inside he found some interesting items. The most important item was a letter. It read as follows:

1254 Peach Street
Ottawa, Ontario T6V 3W4
August 14, 1986

Dear Friend,

If you are reading this letter, you have found my time capsule. My name is Sara Burch and I am eleven years old. I have decided to make a time capsule that holds things that tell about me and about the time I am living in.

I have enclosed a picture of my family. I am the one holding the Cabbage Patch Doll. It was difficult to get this doll because they have become so popular. The piece of string shows you my height. The candy wrapper is from my favourite candies called Jolly Ranchers. These rectangular candies come in the greatest flavours.

The newspaper headline is also very important to this time in history. This year, the space shuttle Challenger exploded as it took off for space. It was a tragic event but it will always be remembered.

I have also enclosed a list of my favourites. As you can see my favourite singer is Madonna. My favourite movie is Ghostbusters and my favourite TV show is called the Care Bears.

I hope you enjoy looking through my time capsule and hopefully you have learned something about the past that you did not know.

Yours truly,
Sara Burch

A. Put a line through the things that were not found in Sara's time capsule.

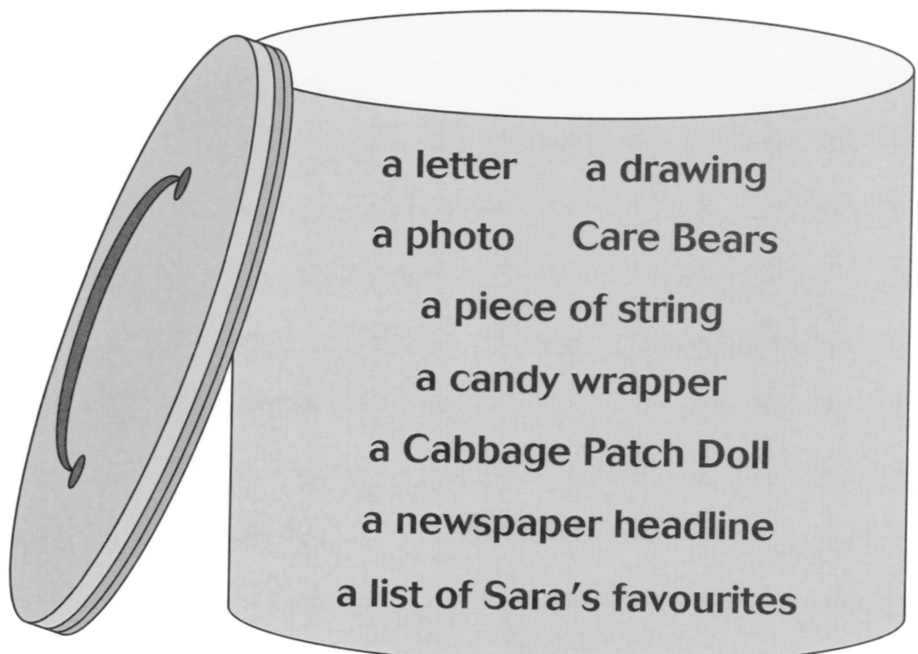

a letter
a drawing
a photo
Care Bears
a piece of string
a candy wrapper
a Cabbage Patch Doll
a newspaper headline
a list of Sara's favourites

B. Complete the crossword puzzle with the antonyms of the clue words. The words can be found in the passage.

Across

A. trivial
B. ordinary
C. joyful
D. boring
E. forgotten

Down

1. hid
2. unpopular

C. Pretend that you are going to make a time capsule. Decide and write what would be important to share with people in the future.

Favourite Toy ______________________

Favourite Singer / Group ______________________

Favourite Movie ______________________

Favourite Food ______________________

Favourite TV Show ______________________

Newspaper Headline ______________________

Other Items ______________________

D. Using Sara's letter as a guide and the list above, write a letter to the person who may find your time capsule.

E. Rewrite each sentence in the past tense.

1. Dad plants the trees in the backyard.

____

2. I need a pen to write the letter.

____

3. My sister plays in the sandbox.

____

4. We laugh at the dog's tricks.

____

5. I follow the path through the forest.

____

Some verbs form the past tense in different ways. They are called ***irregular verbs****.*

F. Match each verb in Column A with its past tense in Column B.

A		B	
1.	drive ____	A.	wrote
2.	dig ____	B.	brought
3.	write ____	C.	bought
4.	fly ____	D.	drank
5.	bring ____	E.	found
6.	drink ____	F.	flew
7.	buy ____	G.	drove
8.	find ____	H.	dug

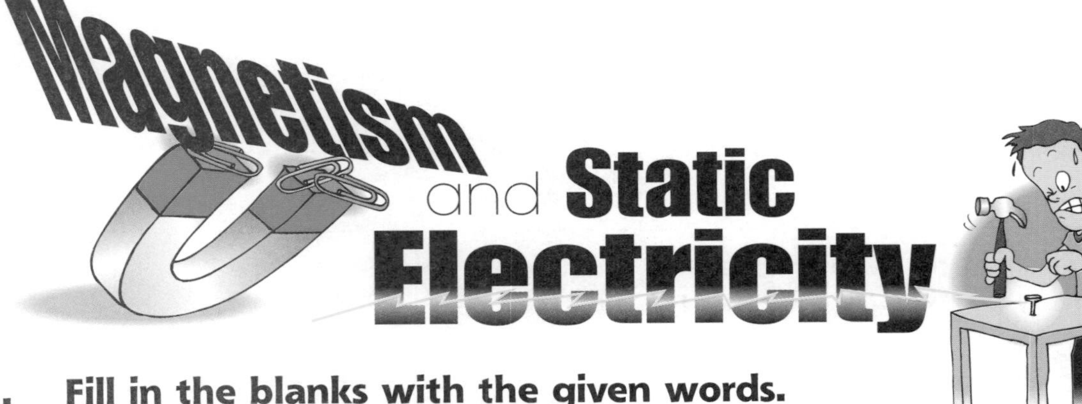

A. Fill in the blanks with the given words.

whales magnetite magnet north south nickel

1. a. The end of the magnet that points to the north is called ______________ pole.

   b. The end of the magnet that points to the south is called ______________ pole.

2. The rock ______________ is a natural magnet, formed deep in the Earth over thousands of years.

3. a. The Earth's core is made mostly from iron and ______________ .

   b. This core makes the Earth act like a huge ______________ .

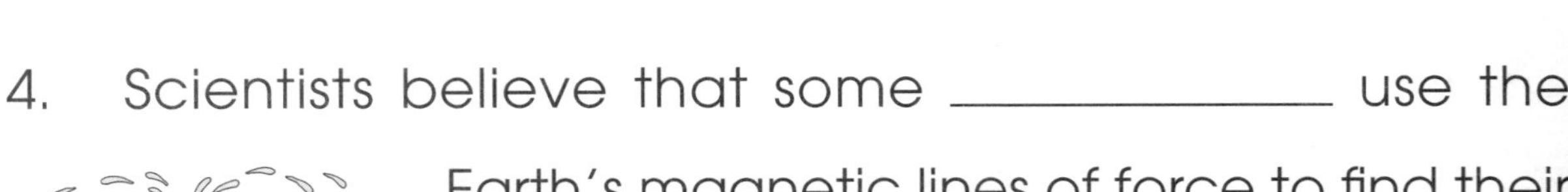

4. Scientists believe that some ______________ use the Earth's magnetic lines of force to find their way in the ocean.

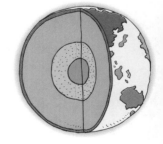

B. Look at the pictures. Check ✔ the things that make use of magnetic forces.

C. Try this!

Forces are everywhere! One of these forces is caused by static electricity. You can explore this invisible force with ease.

- All you need is two balloons, a piece of nylon material, and a piece of wool material.
- Rub the balloons with either the wool or the nylon material. This will "charge" the balloons.
- Try rubbing or not rubbing the balloons with the material and then bring them close together.
- See what happens.

A. Write the capital city beside each province or territory.

1. Alberta ____________________
2. British Columbia ____________________
3. Manitoba ____________________
4. New Brunswick ____________________
5. Newfoundland and Labrador ____________________
6. Northwest Territories ____________________
7. Nova Scotia ____________________
8. Nunavut ____________________
9. Ontario ____________________
10. Prince Edward Island ____________________
11. Quebec ____________________
12. Saskatchewan ____________________
13. Yukon ____________________

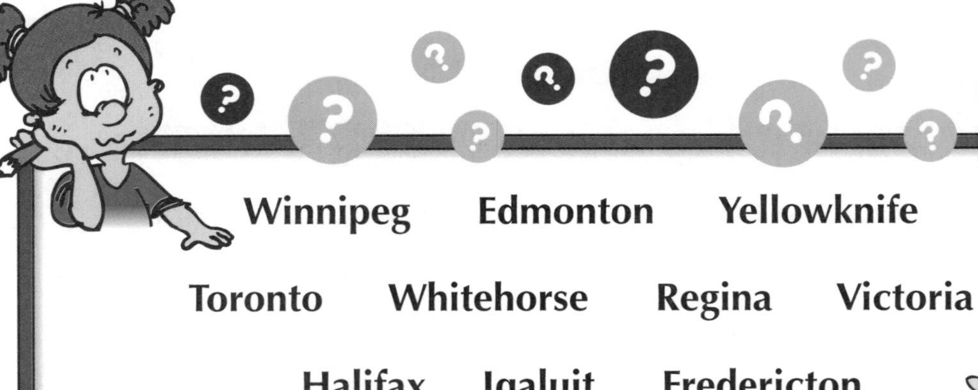

Winnipeg **Edmonton** **Yellowknife**

Toronto **Whitehorse** **Regina** **Victoria**

Halifax **Iqaluit** **Fredericton**

St. John's **Charlottetown** **Québec**

B. Can you guess the provinces or territories? Write their names.

1. I am Canada's newest territory.

   ____

2. I am the smallest province.

   ____

3. I am Canada's largest province.

   ____

4. I have the largest population.

   ____

5. I am often called "Canada's Breadbasket".

   ____

6. I am the territory that reaches farthest north.

   ____

Alberta was named after Princess Louise Caroline Alberta, fourth daughter of Queen Victoria.
About Canada

Week 8

ARTS & CRAFTS

Materials:

- glue
- googly eyes
- pipe cleaners
- magnetic strips
- hole punch
- green foam sheet
- red and orange yarn

Lucky Shamrock People

Directions:

1. Using green foam sheet, trace 1 large and 1 small shamrock per person.
2. Punch 4 holes on large shamrock.
3. Put pipe cleaners through holes and twist.
4. Add googly eyes onto small shamrock.
5. Glue small shamrock over the large one.
6. Cut yarn into short lengths. Tie at centre.
7. Glue to top of shamrock "head".
8. Cut magnetic strip and stick on back of "body".

large
small

ANSWERS

Week 1

Mathematics

A. 1. 81 ; 82 ; 83 ; 84 ; 85
   2. 94 ; 96 ; 98 ; 100 ; 102
   3. 90 ; 95 ; 100 ; 105 ; 110
   4. 75 ; 100 ; 125 ; 150 ; 175
   5. Virginia

B. 1. 500–427 ; 73 ; 73
   2. 273+185 ; 458 ; 458
   3. 400–25 ; 375 ; 375
   4. 577–129 ; 448 ; 448
   5. 415+98 ; 513 ; 513

C. 1. Group 1   2. Group 3
   3. a. 200   b. 500
   4. B

D. 1. Draw 10 cans. ; 15
   2. Draw 9 cans. ; 12

Brain Teaser

8

English

A. 6 ; 3 ; 1 ; 2 ; 8 ; 5 ; 4 ; 7

B. 1. A magician usually wears a top hat.
   2. Rosa's puppy doesn't like cookies.

C. (Individual writing)

D. (Order may vary.)
   1. bedroom
   2. crosswalk
   3. butterfly
   4. lighthouse
   5. downstairs
   6. cookbook
   7. hourglass
   8. sandpit

E. (Individual writing)

Science

A. Pod 1 : leaf ; beetle ; spider ; bird ; cat
   Pod 2 : clover ; grasshopper ; frog ; snake ; hawk
   Pod 3 : plankton ; water insect ; minnow ; large mouth bass ; osprey

B.

	[A] H	E	R	B	I	V	[3] O	R	E		
[1] C							M				
O					[2] P		N			[4] P	
N			[B] C	A	R	N	I	V	O	R	E
S					E		V			E	
U					Y		O			D	
M							R			A	
[C] E	C	O	S	Y	S	T	E	M		T	
R										O	
			[D] P	R	O	D	U	C	E	R	

Social Studies

A. 1. Cree
   2. Ojibway
   3. Innu
   4. Algonquin
   5. Wendat
   6. Iroquois

B.

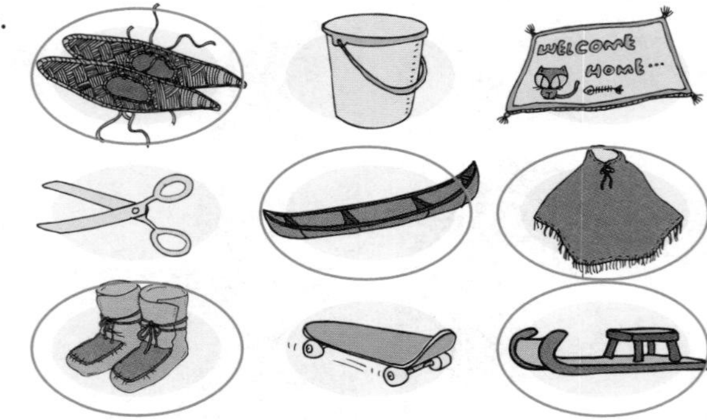

C. 1. ✔   2. ✔
   3.   4. ✔
   5. ✔   6.

Week 2

Mathematics

A. 1. A : 9:15 a.m.
      B : 8:15 p.m.
      C : 8:30 a.m.
      D : 9:30 p.m.
      E : $2.25
      F : $3.06
   2. 11 hours
   3. 13 hours
   4. $8.37

B. 1. 9 ; 50 ; 9.50 ; C

2. 51 ; 22 ; 51.22 ; B
3. 100 ; 25 ; 100.25 ; C

C. 1. 4.45+3.15 = 7.60 ; 7.60
2. 10–2.28–2.59 = 5.13 ; 5.13
3. 1.98+1.98+1.98–1.19 = 4.75 ; 4.75

D. 1. 36 2. 141
3. 102 4. 32

Brain Teaser

5

English

A. 1. T 2. F
3. F 4. T
5. T

B. 1. Mud Puddle was the first book that Robert Munsch had published.
2. Peter read his class a story called Get out of Bed.
3. Charlotte's Web is a novel about a friendship between a pig and a spider.
4. Love You Forever became a bestseller in Canada.

C.

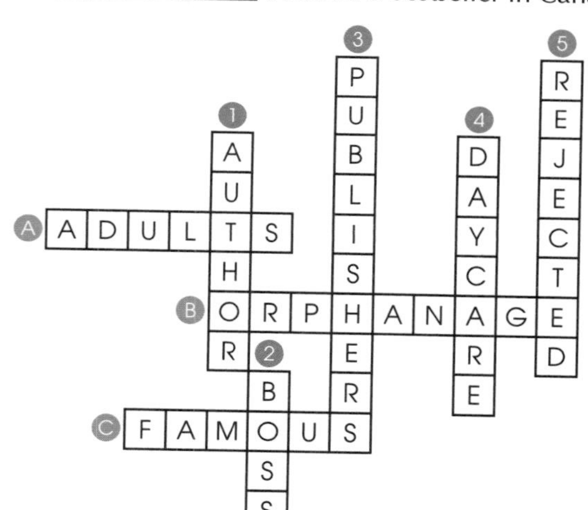

D. 1. Andrew's Loose Tooth
2. Angela's Airplane
3. Get out of Bed
4. I Have to Go
5. Millicent and the Wind
6. Mortimer
7. Stephanie's Ponytail
8. The Fire Station

E. (Individual questions)

Science

A. 1. flower 2. seed
3. leaf 4. stem
5. roots

B. (Individual observation)

C. 1. plants 2. trunk
3. nutrients / water 4. water / nutrients
5. leaves 6. branches
7. bark

D. 1. energy 2. water
3. light 4. air
5. nutrients
(Order of 2, 3, and 4 may vary.)

Social Studies

A. 1. ✔ 2. ✔
3. ✘ 4. ✘
5. ✔ 6. ✘
7. ✘

B. 1. Scotland
2. England
3. Germany
4. Atlantic Ocean
5. St. Lawrence River
6. Italy

Week 3

Mathematics

A. 1. 5 2. 8
3. 8 4. 5
5. 3

B. 1. 2.62 ; 2.38 2. 1.81 ; 0.19
3. 2.73 ; 0.27 4. 4.49 ; 0.51
5. 5.32 ; 4.68

C. 1. 180 ; 80 2. 190 ; 20
3. 230 ; 14 4. 160 ; 50
5. 200 ; 15

D. 1. 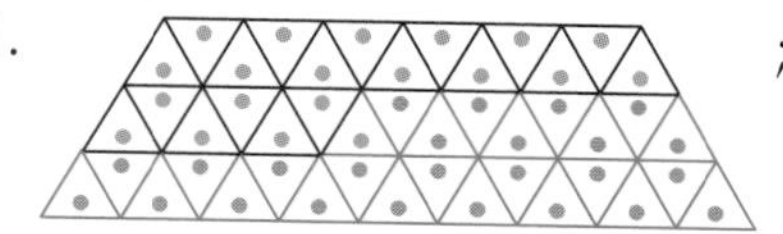 ; 934 ; 29

2.  ; 49 ; 28

3. ; 372 ; 22

Math Game

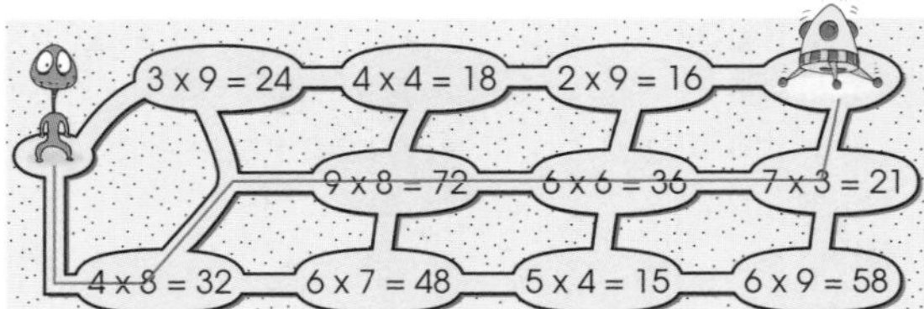

English

A. (Individual drawing and writing)
B. (Individual lists of words)
C. (Individual writing)
D. (Individual writing)
E. (Suggested answers)
   1. Julia's mother asked Vanessa and Nadia, "Would you like to stay for dinner?"
   2. "I have a surprise for you all," Julia's mother told the girls.
   3. "Let's make friendship bracelets for one another," Julia sugguested.
   4. Julia asked her mother, "Could we have pizza for dinner?"
   5. "Mom, it's the best day ever," Julia said.

Science

A. 1. B 2. C
B. Wind pollinated : C, D
   Insect pollinated : A, B, E
C. 1. B 2. D
   3. F 4. A
   5. C 6. E

Social Studies

A. 1. B 2. A
   3. C 4. B
   5. A 6. B

Challenge

Popcorn

B. 1. bark ; tea
   2. maple ; syrup
   3. poplar ; tonic
   4. Birch ; canoes
C. (Suggested answers)
   1. 2. ✘ 3. ✘
   4. 5. 6. ✘
   7. ✘ 8. 9. ✘
   10. ✘

Week 4

Mathematics

A. 1. 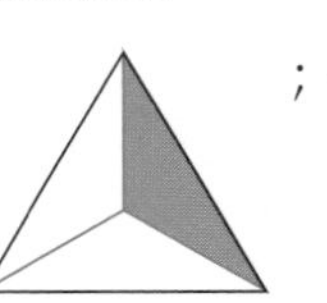 ; $\frac{1}{3}$

2.  ; $\frac{1}{2}$

3. 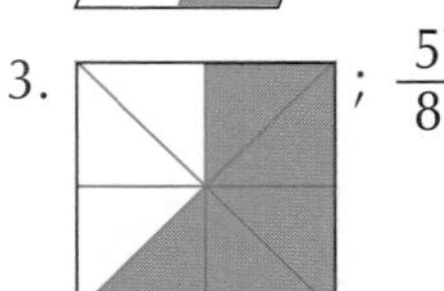 ; $\frac{5}{8}$

4. 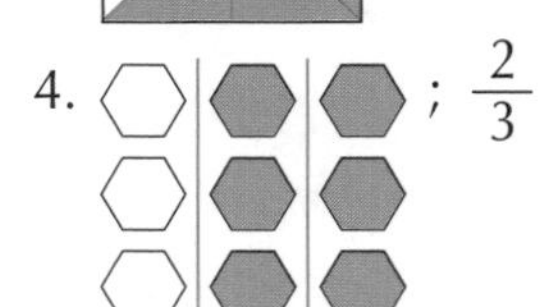 ; $\frac{2}{3}$

5.  ; $\frac{2}{3}$

B. 1. Triangle ; 3 ; 3
   2. Parallelogram ; 4 ; 4
   3. Square ; 4 ; 4
   4. Hexagon ; 6 ; 6
   5. Rhombus ; 4 ; 4

C. 1.
   2.
   3.

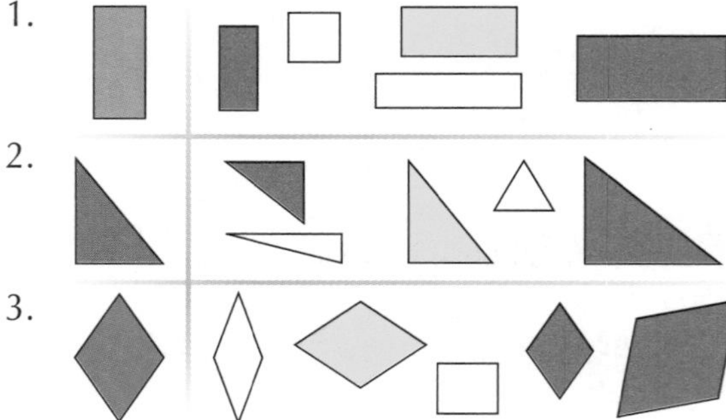

D. 1. Tiffany 2. 80
   3. Ivy 4. 50
   5. Patrick 6. John
   7. 3 8. 50

E.

		Reflection Image	Translation Image	Rotation Image
1.				
2.				
3.				
4.				
5.				

Brain Teaser

6

English

A. 1. The Emperor Penguin has a black bill with a yellow-orange streak.
   2. Emperor Penguins live in Antarctica.
   3. The brood pouch keeps the egg safe and warm.
   4. Chicks could freeze to death within two minutes.
   5. Baby penguins take two months or so to hatch.
   6. The penguins huddle together in a huge group.

B.

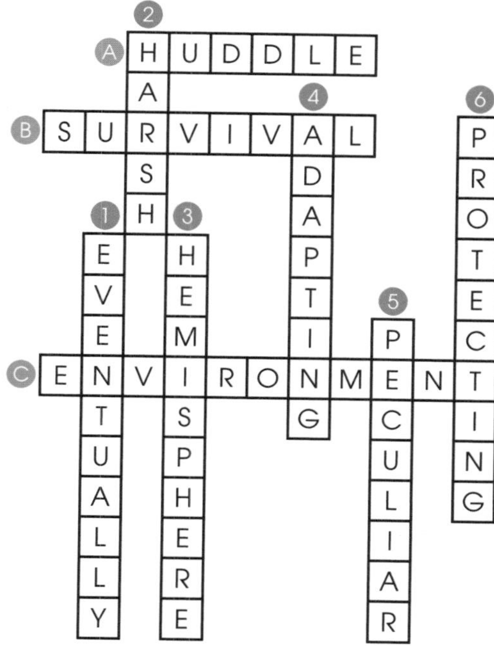

C. (Individual writing)

D. icebergers

Science

A. (Individual answers)

B. 1. N 2. A
   3. N 4. N
   5. A 6. A

C. (Individual answers)

Social Studies

A. (Suggested answers)
   1. ✔ 2. ✔
   3. 4.
   5. 6. ✔
   7. ✔ 8.

Challenge

(Individual writing)

B. 1. B 2. A
   3. B 4. C
   5. A 6. C

Challenge

B

Week 5

Mathematics

A. (Suggested answers)

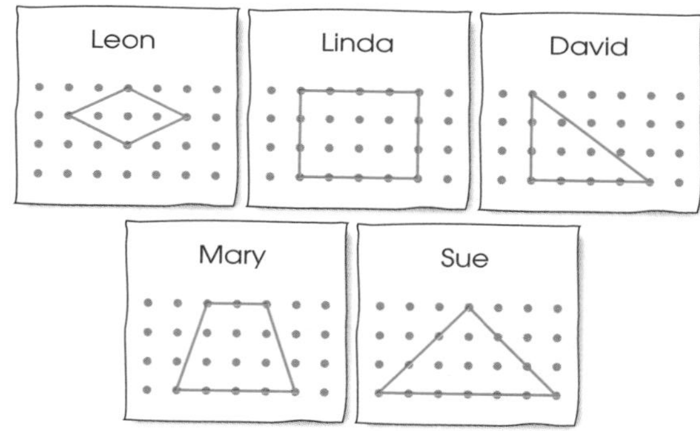

B. 1. Triangular prism ; 5
   2. Rectangular pyramid ; 5
   3. Triangular pyramid ; 4
   4. Hexagonal prism ; 8
   5. Pentagonal pyramid ; 6
   6. Rectangular prism ; 6
   7. Square-based pyramid ; 5

C. 1. ; 12
   2. ; 8

3.  ; 12

4.  ; 12

D. 1. 80 ; 90 ; 50 ; 30 ; 60
   2. eighty
   3. ninety
   4. fifty
   5. thirty
   6. sixty

Math Game

D

English

A. 1.
   2. ✔
   3. ✔
   4. ✔
   5.
   6.

B. (Individual answers)

C. (Individual writing)

D.

g	r	y	m	l	z	n	v	w	a	n	u	p	h	y	c
u	o	a	t	b	l	a	g	v	s	k	a	w	w	i	r
b	l	r	d	x	e	s	y	p	t	j	t	t	h	o	e
x	l	e	s	r	b	k	s	v	t	y	s	r	e	q	a
o	e	z	b	o	m	a	r	a	r	n	u	i	e	x	v
q	r	m	w	l	q	t	u	n	i	c	y	c	l	e	s
h	s	i	m	l	z	e	m	v	g	w	l	y	b	d	y
y	k	p	o	g	a	b	x	b	t	p	k	c	a	m	h
e	a	u	t	o	m	o	b	i	l	e	t	l	r	q	c
p	t	h	o	q	d	a	s	c	o	o	t	e	r	n	g
o	e	w	r	z	o	r	y	y	i	l	w	i	o	s	f
c	s	j	c	a	m	d	r	c	u	j	o	v	w	t	l
x	d	s	y	v	f	x	q	l	s	w	a	g	o	n	e
a	v	o	c	t	m	g	w	e	z	x	o	y	d	x	s
m	r	o	l	l	e	r	b	l	a	d	e	s	j	v	a
l	s	b	e	t	p	n	o	g	r	l	m	g	w	b	r
u	i	r	z	k	b	c	w	i	u	a	z	f	t	l	v

Science

A. 1. stable
   2. unstable
   3. stable
   4. unstable
   5. unstable
   6. stable
   7. unstable

B. 1. Squeeze
   2. Twist
   3. Stretch
   4. Bend
   5. Slide

Social Studies

A. (Suggested answers)
   1. Different
   2. Different
   3. Different
   4. Different
   5. Different
   6. Different
   7. Different
   8. Same
   9. Different
   10. Same

B. 1. Hopscotch
   2. Marbles
   3. Spinning Tops
   4. Sack Races
   5. Hoops
   6. Tic Tac Toe

   (Individual colouring)

Week 6

Mathematics

A. 1. A : Triangular prism
   B : Cube
   C : Cylinder
   D : Triangular pyramid
   E : Rectangular prism
   F : Hexagonal pyramid
   G : Pentagonal prism

2. A
3. D
4. 5
5. 3
6. 3

B. 1. 3.87
2. 0.42
3. 1.16
4. 0.38
5. 0.80
6. 2.08
7. 1.02
8. 4.29
9. 2.92
10. 4

C. 1. a. 42 ; 38 ; 34
b. 26
2. a. 16 ; 24 ; 32 ; 40 ; 48
b. 64
3. a. 10 ; 15 ; 20
b. 30

D. 1. a. Colour any 8 packets.
b. 8
2. a. Colour any 5 packets.
b. 5

Brain Teaser

1. $\frac{1}{3}$ 2. $\frac{1}{4}$ 3. $\frac{2}{3}$

English

A. 1. Her mother said it was too dangerous.
2. She couldn't swim across the pool.
3. It is the tallest mountain in the world.
4. (Any one of these things)
She went camping / stayed in a cottage on Pigeon Lake for a week.
She spent an entire day at Canada's Wonderland.
She spent many hours with her friends rollerblading, biking, hiking, and splashing in the pool.
5. (Individual answer)

B. 1. vacation
2. miss
3. biking
4. created
5. coach
6. entire
7. tallest
8. dangerous

C. (Individual lists)

D. (Individual writing)

E. 1. I can't play street hockey this afternoon.
2. Maria couldn't find her sunglasses.
3. I've read stories about Mount Everest.
4. It's wonderful to sleep in during the week.
5. We're going to go camping in Algonquin Park.

F. (Individual writing and drawings)

Science

A. rock, air, water, humus

B. (Individual observation)

C.

a	w	o	l	j	e	m	i	g	c	r	b	o
c	o	f	f	e	e	g	r	o	u	n	d	s
w	p	v	e	g	e	t	a	b	l	e	s	p
e	l	d	w	g	r	a	s	s	r	h	o	q
j	a	f	h	s	k	g	a	s	y	l	i	m
t	n	s	b	h	c	f	r	u	i	t	l	w
x	t	j	t	e	a	b	a	g	s	p	y	b
u	s	a	e	l	e	a	v	e	s	x	c	l
o	h	g	i	l	f	w	r	q	k	m	a	c
b	y	t	r	s	a	d	i	b	e	g	f	k

Social Studies

A.

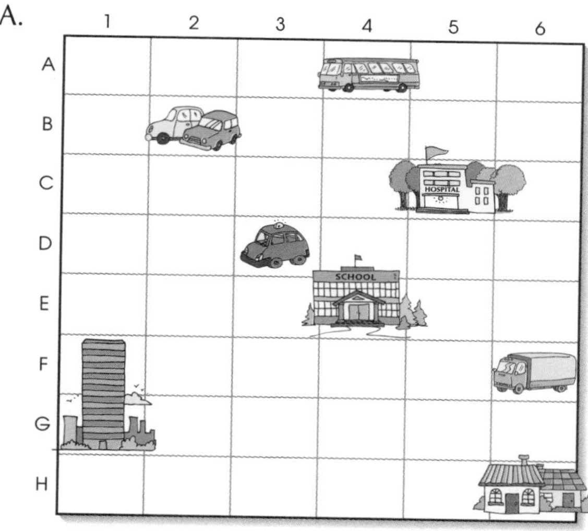

B.

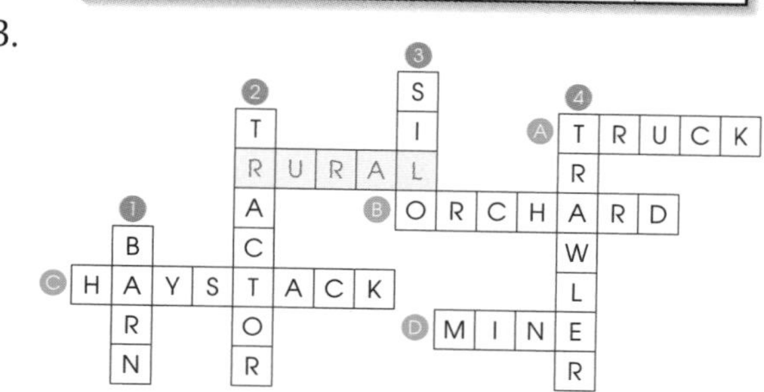

Week 7

Mathematics

A. 1. 4.60 ; 2.44 ; 1.09 ;
0.95 ; 3.49 ; 2.89
2. \$5.55 ; \$0.45
3. \$4.58 ; \$1.42
4. \$7.77 ; \$2.23

B. 1.

213	30	99	90	63	22	25	55	40
552	10	43	35	108	49	68	84	85
92	20	15	5	70	457	75	45	60
56	32	72	80	503	9	100	752	37
27	356	102	65	6	207	95	50	105

;

761 ; 624 ; 42 ; 162

2.

13	11	16	81	24	30	42	31	3
55	73	4	11	2	13	83	61	43
17	99	8	27	10	6	28	79	87
73	67	20	35	14	37	44	13	9
49	51	12	5	38	26	50	67	15

;

30 ; 14 ; 36 ; 24

3.

72	66	32	10	50	40	2	26	42
5	48	13	25	22	60	52	47	8
23	17	84	30	70	80	63	54	93
45	28	62	20	36	31	7	15	72
87	96	36	150	100	90	14	67	39

;

615 ; 344 ; 470 ; 717

4. A

C. 1. 9 ; 36
2. 8 ; 36 ; $\frac{8}{36}$
3. 12 ; 36 ; $\frac{12}{36}$
4. 8
5. 4
6. 8
7. 18

D. 1. 70 ; 65 ; 60 ; 55
2. 38 ; 36 ; 34 ; 32
3. 150 ; 175 ; 200 ; 225
4. 230 ; 240 ; 250 ; 260
5. decreases ; 5
6. decreases ; 2
7. increases ; 25
8. increases ; 10

Math Game

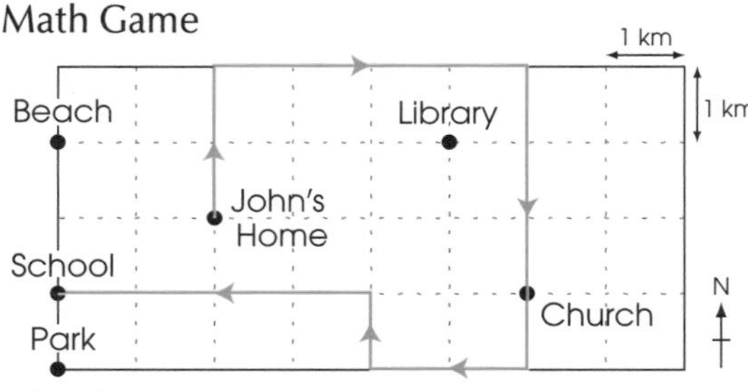

school

English

A. 1. It was a very bumpy ride but it was all worth it.
2. It was very easy to get lost in the old, enormous building.
3. A large silver suit of armour at the end of a long corridor caught his attention.
4. Larry felt his hand moving toward the doorknob.

B. 1. The teacher said, "The castle is very old and historic."
2. "Let's go into this room," shouted Larry.
3. "How long will the bus ride be?" asked the class.
4. "I enjoyed the trip," said Brian.
5. The bus driver declared, "We are almost at the castle."

C. (Individual writing and drawing)

D.

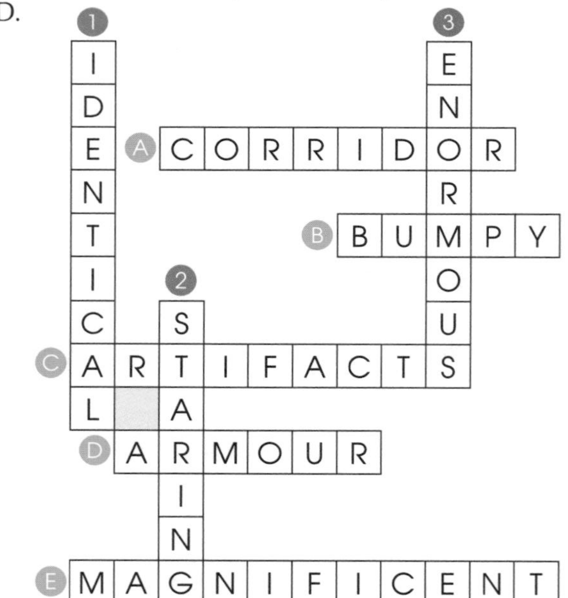

Science

A. 1. friction
 2. less
 3. rough
 4. more
 5. force
B. (Suggested answers)
 4 ; 5 ; 2 ; 1 ; 3
C. 1. grip
 2. slip
 3. grip
 4. slip
 5. slip
 6. grip
 7. slip
 8. grip

Social Studies

A. 1. Great Britain
 2. government
 3. independent
 4. Dominion
 5. provinces
 6. ten
 7. three
 8. Canada Day
B. 1. British Columbia
 2. Alberta
 3. Manitoba
 4. Ontario
 5. Quebec
 6. Nova Scotia
 7. New Brunswick
 8. Saskatchewan
 9. Newfoundland and Labrador
 10. Prince Edward Island
 11. Northwest Territories
 12. Yukon
 13. Nunavut
C. (Individual writing)

Week 8

Mathematics

A. 1. impossible
 2. impossible
 3. possible
 4. possible
 5. impossible
 6. possible
B. 1. ✘ 2. ✔
 3. ✘ 4. ✘
 5. ✔ 6. ✔
 7. ✘ 8. ✔
C. 1. Colour 5 marbles green, 4 marbles yellow, and 3 marbles red.
 2. Yes
 3. No
 4. A green marble
 5. A yellow marble
 6. Green
 7. 6 marbles
 8. 1st Group : 2 ;
 2nd Group : 3 ; 3
 1st Group : 4 yellow, 1 green, 1 red ;
 2nd Group : 4 green, 2 red
 1st Group : 4 yellow, 2 red ;
 2nd Group : 5 green, 1 red
D. 1. 60 2. 35
 3. 45 4. 20

Math Game

3, 7, 11, 12, 15, 16, 20, 21, 25, and 30

English

A.

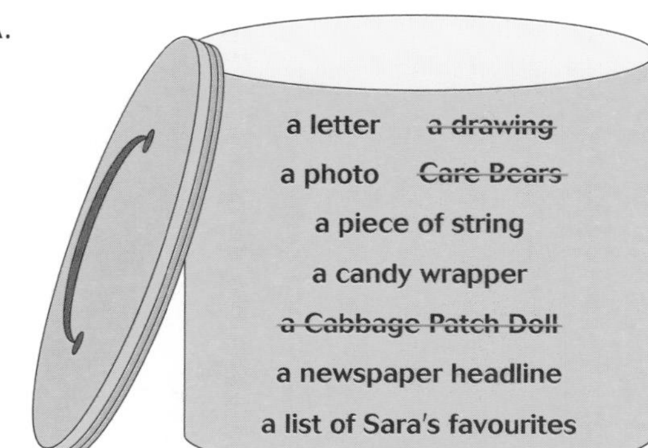

a letter
~~a drawing~~
a photo
~~Care Bears~~
a piece of string
a candy wrapper
~~a Cabbage Patch Doll~~
a newspaper headline
a list of Sara's favourites

B.

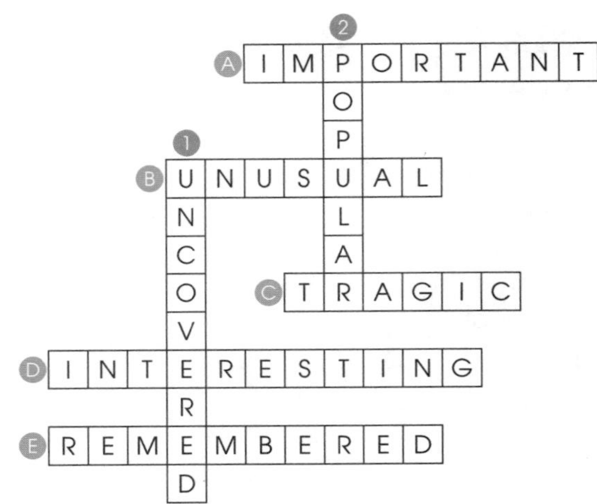

C. (Individual writing)

D. (Individual writing)

E. 1. Dad planted the trees in the backyard.
 2. I needed a pen to write the letter.
 3. My sister played in the sandbox.
 4. We laughed at the dog's tricks.
 5. I followed the path through the forest.

F. 1. G 2. H
 3. A 4. F
 5. B 6. D
 7. C 8. E

Science

A. 1. a. north b. south
 2. magnetite
 3. a. nickel b. magnet
 4. whales

B. Check pictures A, C, and E.

C. (Individual observation)

Social Studies

A. 1. Edmonton
 2. Victoria
 3. Winnipeg
 4. Fredericton
 5. St. John's
 6. Yellowknife
 7. Halifax
 8. Iqaluit
 9. Toronto
 10. Charlottetown
 11. Québec
 12. Regina
 13. Whitehorse

B. 1. Nunavut
 2. Prince Edward Island
 3. Quebec
 4. Ontario
 5. Saskatchewan
 6. Nunavut

My Lovely Napkin Rings

Cut out the napkin rings. Decide who you are going to give these rings to. Then write a sentence on the line to make each napkin special.

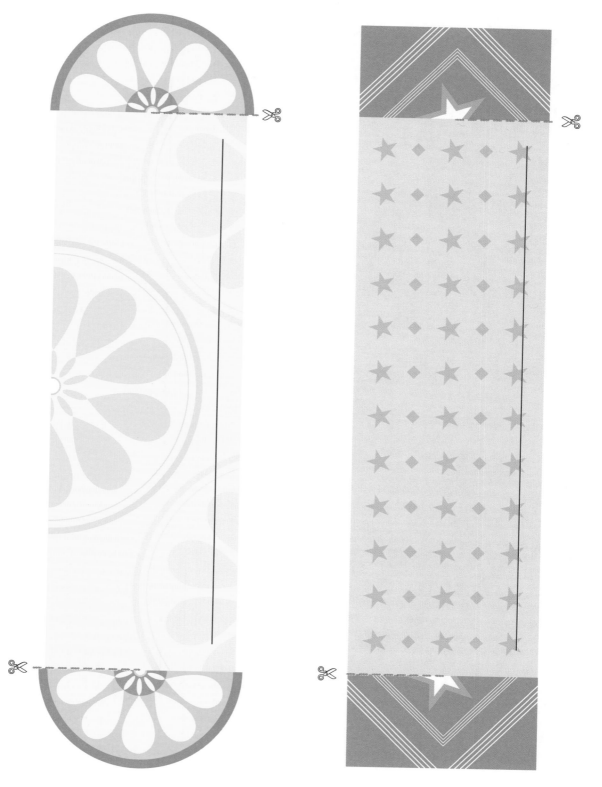

Flower Words

Cut out the flower. Then cut out the "petals" with the names of flowers and glue them on the flower.

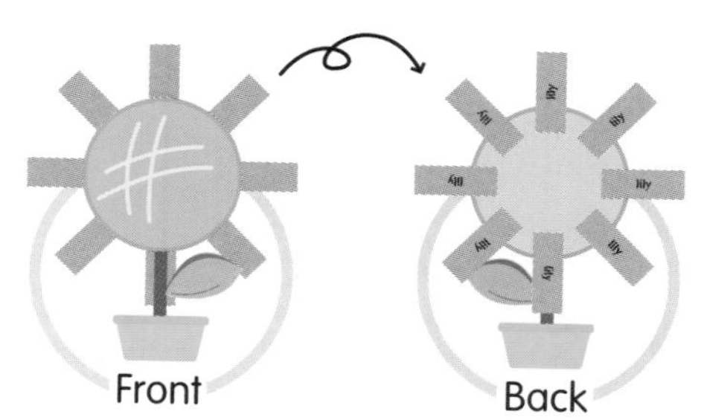

tulip

lemon

rose

daisy

basil

sunflower

purple

carnation

weed

daffodil

lily

lilac

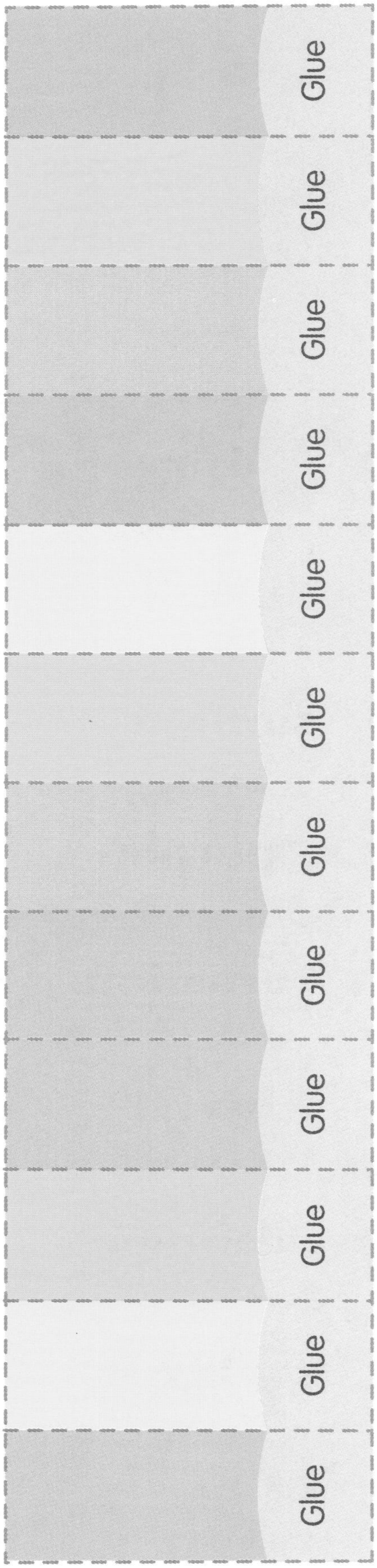
Glue
Glue
Glue
Glue
Glue
Glue
Glue
Glue
Glue
Glue
Glue
Glue

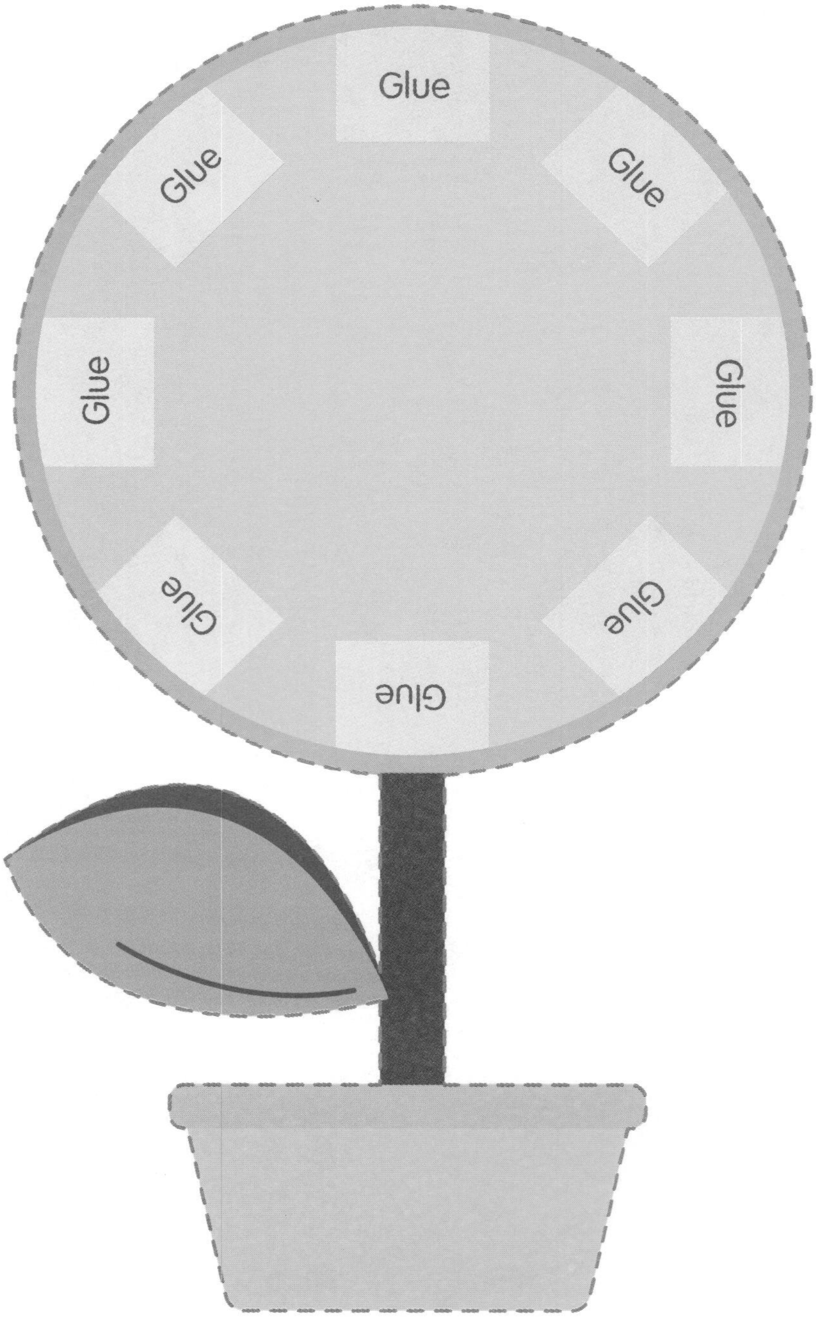
Glue
Glue
Glue
Glue
Glue
Glue
Glue
Glue

Trace the dotted lines and follow the pattern to draw and colour the shapes. Cut out the net of the party hat. Then glue it.

Glue

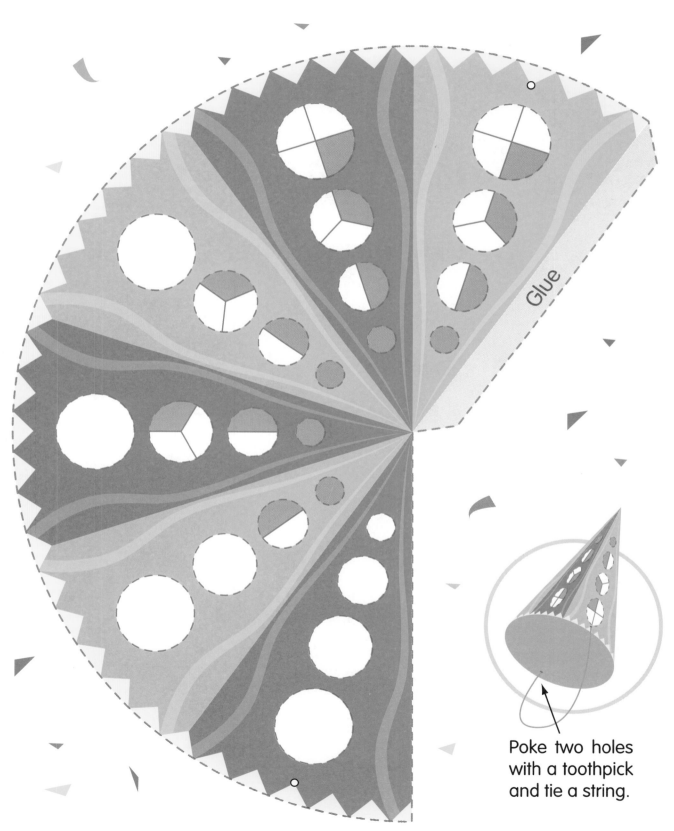

Poke two holes with a toothpick and tie a string.

3-D Puzzles

Cut out the nets for the cubes. Glue the tabs of each cube. Then stack the cubes to see what pictures you can get.

Yo!

Hello!

How are you?

Glue

Glue

Glue

Good morning!

Hi!

Shh!

Glue

Glue

Glue

Glue

Glue

Glue

Glue

Glue

Glue

Glue

Glue

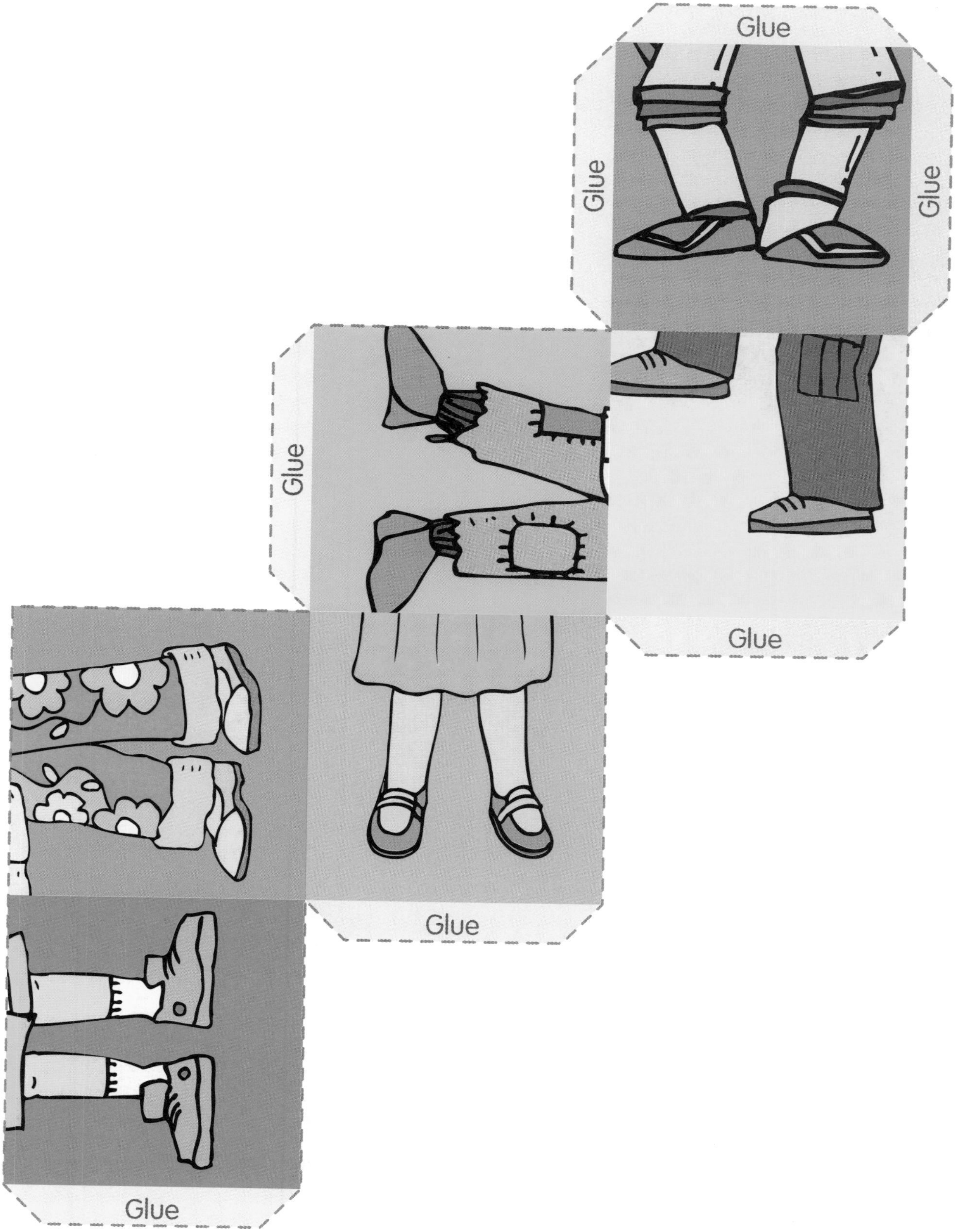

Glue

Glue

Glue

Glue

Glue

Glue

Glue

Glue

A Snowflake

Cut out the square. Follow the steps to fold along the red lines. Then cut along the dotted yellow line. Open it. You have made a beautiful snowflake.

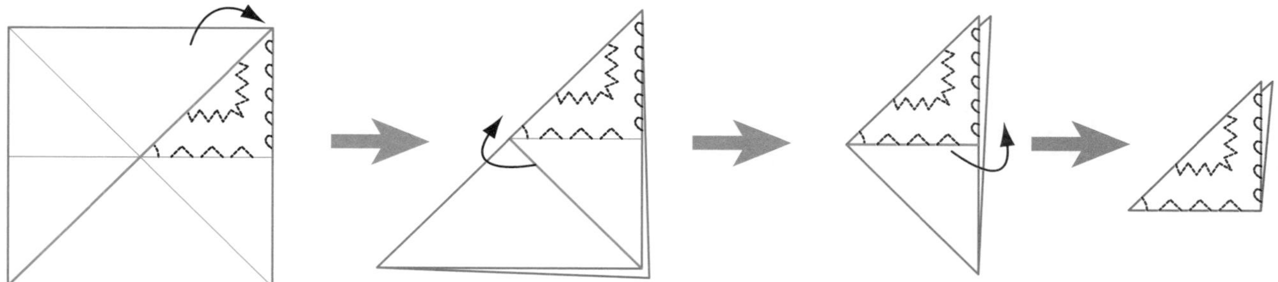

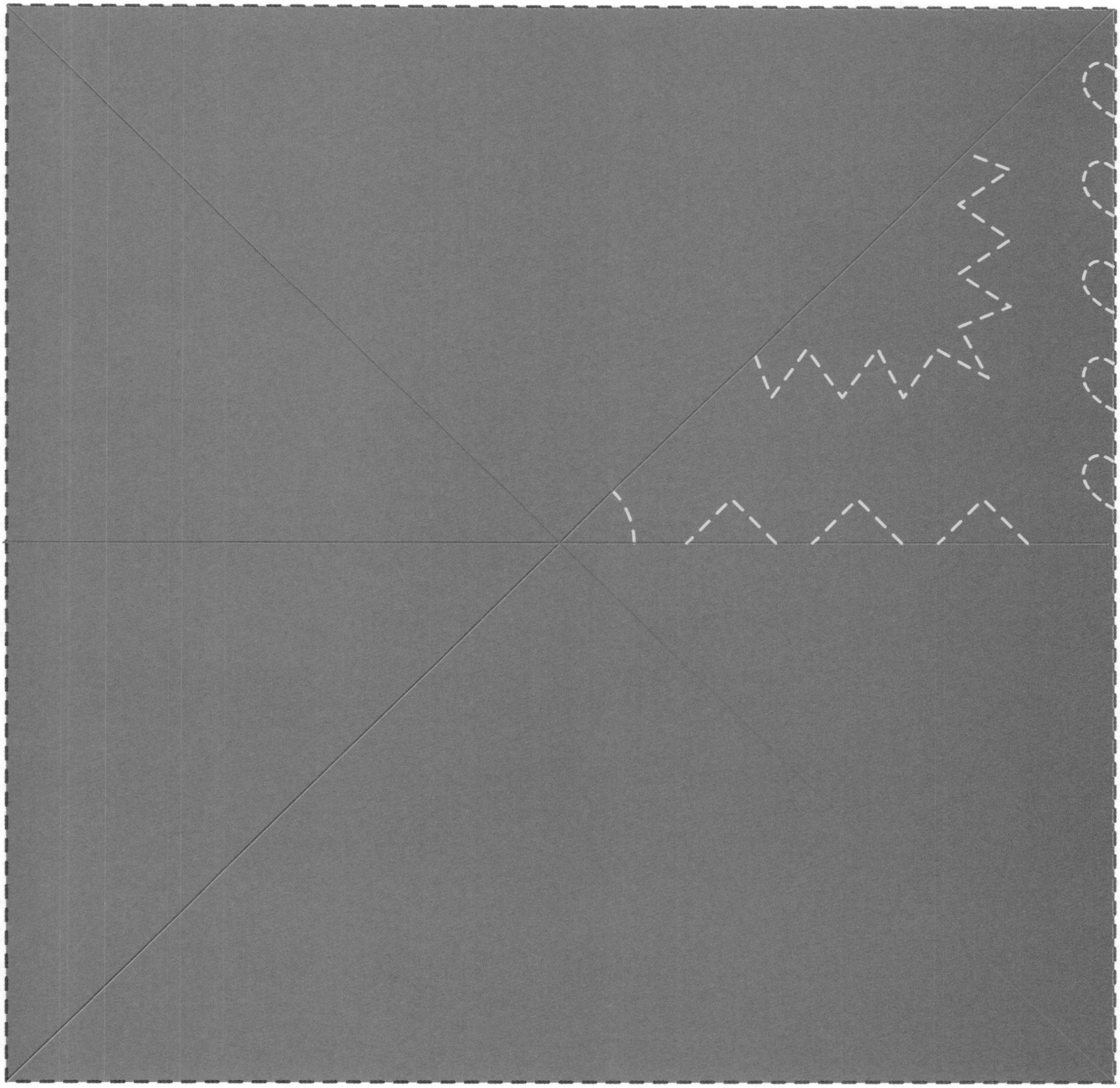

A Bookmark

Complete the reflection image on the right. Cut, fold, and glue the bookmark. Then poke a hole in the bookmark and tie a string or ribbon.

Fold here

Glue

Glue

Story Fun

Cut out the pieces. Place them face down on the table. Draw 3 pieces and give them to your buddy. Ask your buddy to make up a story with the pictures. Then let your buddy pick 3 pieces for you and now it is your turn to tell a story.